T0022910

You Were Watching from the Sand

You Were Watching from the Sand

short stories

Juliana Lamy

2021
Ann Petry Award

Red Hen Press | *Pasadena, CA*

Book layout by Rebeccah Sanhueza

Library of Congress Cataloging-in-Publication Data

Names: Lamy, Juliana, 1998– author.
Title: You were watching from the sand: short stories / Juliana Lamy.
Other titles: You were watching from the sand (Compilation)
Description: Pasadena, CA: Red Hen Press, [2023]
Identifiers: LCCN 2023018716 (print) | LCCN 2023018717 (ebook) | ISBN
  9781636281056 (paperback) | ISBN 9781636281063 (ebook)
Subjects: LCSH: Haitians—Fiction. | LCGFT: Short stories.
Classification: LCC PS3612.A54746 Y68 2023 (print) | LCC PS3612.A54746
  (ebook) | DDC 813/.6—dc23/eng/20230503
LC record available at https://lccn.loc.gov/2023018716
LC ebook record available at https://lccn.loc.gov/2023018717

The National Endowment for the Arts, the Los Angeles County Arts Commission, the Ahmanson Foundation, the Dwight Stuart Youth Fund, the Max Factor Family Foundation, the Pasadena Tournament of Roses Foundation, the Pasadena Arts & Culture Commission and the City of Pasadena Cultural Affairs Division, the City of Los Angeles Department of Cultural Affairs, the Audrey & Sydney Irmas Charitable Foundation, the Meta & George Rosenberg Foundation, the Albert and Elaine Borchard Foundation, the Adams Family Foundation, Amazon Literary Partnership, the Sam Francis Foundation, and the Mara W. Breech Foundation partially support Red Hen Press.

First Edition
Published by Red Hen Press
www.redhen.org

For my parents and my brothers,
and a fourfold love.

Contents

You Were Watching from the Sand

You Were Watching from the Sand

"Of course I remember you. You were born on one of those days where the sky won't break apart for the rain, where the sky won't break apart for the sun. You were born on one of those days where everybody's bone-tired, where sleep drags through them and replaces the blood, and all the branches of Exhaustion the River empty out inside their stomachs. When everybody has a lake with them, right under the heaven of their ribs. Those days where you could drown if you stayed too long inside yourself.

You were born on one of those days where people forget how to drive, where people know, for themselves, when to change lanes, but forget that no one else knows what's about to happen. Where all the things happening inside their heads feel like they fell in when the world cracked open and its heart and its lungs spilled out. Where the only planet that ever existed or will exist is the one they're looking out at right now, the one with gray asphalt strapped to the surface, the one with those huge green signs coming up out of the ground telling them that they're *five exits away from the closest Wendy's.* The one with all those speed limit markers that they ignore because you can go as fast as you want in the world you want to see.

Listen, you were born on one of those days where the air was for breathing, for sitting outside your house with your eyes closed or open or watching, for walking to the store instead of taking the car, for letting your kids run around in the grass green like health, like life, like living. Run around because they couldn't find Exhaustion the River inside them yet.

You were born on one of those days school was out. Not the weekend, but something just like it, where no one *had* to do anything, and freedom tore itself open so that anybody in that town could walk through it. It was a holiday. I remember which one, but that's not what you came here to hear, is it? No, you need to know that you were born on a quiet day. Not quiet like silent, but quiet like calm, quiet like beauty, quiet like serenity, quiet like love, quiet like those things that come into you and live there, steady. Stay with you until you get it, until you know that they're never leaving. Until you *get it*, know that you can always find them when you really need them. When those kids bully you for being too skinny, when you're so angry it starts running down your cheeks, makes everybody think you're crying when you know you're not. When your dad leaves, when Frankie breaks your PlayStation. When you lose those five bucks, when Liza wins the Golden Star in fifth grade, the one you knew belonged to you. When your dad dies, when you can't find the sneakers you want to wear to your first day of seventh grade. When the pain runs so hot up and down and through you, when you're thinking that the only thing that could fix this Bad Thing that you're feeling is a Worse Thing. When Eden cuts you in the cafeteria line and grabs the last stick of French toast, when Ms. Ponte from ninth-grade history tries to convince you that Christopher Columbus landed on Hispaniola first when you *know* for a fact that he landed on the Bahamas way before he ever made it that far south. When you get home that day and your mom looks up at you, more nervous than you've ever seen her (have you ever seen her nervous? You don't think so), and you're scared even before she says it. Even before she tells you about the Black angels with hair like white light, the ones she keeps seeing in the living room right next to the TV, right next to the coffee table. When you barely make it through eleventh grade, even though your SAT scores came out so high that Ms. Roll from the guidance office is throwing around these words, these names, these things like *Columbia* and *NYU* and *Yale*. But she doesn't get it, she doesn't get that you're your own static sea, that *Emory* and *Harvard* and *Stanford* are so heavy that they're not gonna float, that they could never keep themselves above the surface of you. That they're gonna sink to the bottom, to the dark, to the cold. When Frankie gets some girl pregnant and they run off together, your baby brother, gone. When it breaks your mom, splits her in half, when you come home a few days after Frankie leaves and she's turned on all the gas stoves, flames so hot they're blue and you're thinking for a second, *just* for one second *we're in the throat of a star*. When you turn them all off, when you find your mom in her room, in the tiniest tightest little ball in that corner next to her bedside table, trying to make you understand that *the angels told her to do it, the house is gonna flood, god said he'd never end the world like this again but he lied*. When you don't get her help, when you don't tell anyone because you're scared, you're so scared that if you give somebody your mom they're never, ever going to give her back. When you stay after school that day because Mr. Tate tells you he needs to talk to you about your lab report. When you get there and he locks the door, closes the windows, crowds around you, becomes your ceiling, your floor, your walls because you're skinny, remember? You were never big like Frankie. When he pushes you up against the graduated cylinders when he takes off your pants when you feel him inside you was it his hand or something else? You can't remember, you don't know, you don't know, you don't know because before it even started you'd left your body behind, you'd swam to the shore. You were watching it happen from the sand, some tiny Black boy with a face as blank as the rest of the universe, eyes so empty you couldn't believe they'd ever been anything but. When it was done, in those seconds minutes hours days weeks that chased that lifetime next to the graduated cylinders, in all that time that unspooled behind that forever between the Erlenmeyer flasks like cable wire, like twine, like rope you wanted to cinch tight around the world's throat. When you don't get You help, because you felt in the deepest, most invisible pieces of your soul, somewhere inside that black dense forest, between those huge trees that stood like people on the brown earth of you, that if you got help, you'd lose that Kid for real. The one between the beakers, the one bent over the lab table, the one you already couldn't find. You already couldn't find him but you'd never admit that to anyone, you'd die before you did, and I was the only one who ever knew he was already gone. You thought that if you told somebody, you'd give them that You, and they were never, ever going to give him back. When you ask your mom to switch schools and in one of her moments of clarity, beautiful but disappearing already, like a shooting star in a short-lived tumble across the sky's black face, she agrees. She agrees and she doesn't ask why because she's staring through the cracks of the mausoleum you're already trying to stick your pain inside. She's staring at it hard and in its face, watching it crack the walls of its tomb, watching it stab holes into its roof, watching it watch her. When you move to Rainier High, across town. When you don't notice the muddy puddle outside your car and you step in it. That October, when you trip over a JanSport some girl left in the aisle in Stat. When you're a senior now, when the guidance counselor here starts throwing all those heavy things at you too, unbelievably dense singularities that fall to the bottom of you. When you meet that girl with the huge sleepy brown eyes. That girl who takes her naps in the back of sixth period Physics, but could knock out a pulley question no problem in the 3.2 seconds she's actually awake in class. The one that liked you, the one that you liked, the one that made that heavy thick sound crash around the concrete room your head became (the one with walls hard enough for somebody to break themselves against). That sound that was you laughing, and it surprised you because you'd forgotten, really. You'd forgotten that the sounds that came from you didn't always have to be forced, didn't always have to be like throwing a tin bucket down a well to try to catch whatever was left of the water down there, always always *always* hearing it scratch against that hard rock right under you. You forgot that laughing could be easy, like breathing, like blinking, like *being* before that eternity in front of the beakers. When you get green grass streaks on your white sneakers while you're running across the football field to meet her. When she kisses you under the bleachers, just as the shot-put throwers are running past to practice. When you start looking forward to every beat of your heart inside your chest again. When she's driving drunk one night, when she hits that forty-year-old woman walking at the intersection of Cedar and Main, when the woman's church program falls into the gutter, when November comes and that girl moves away. When every single new morning starts sitting on your chest again, when the world loses focus, when it slides back into the cosmic blackness it came from. When you get home from your last day of school before Christmas break and you can't find your mom. When you walk all around the house, through the living room, through the kitchen, through her room, through yours, and you don't see her. When you go out to the backyard and something tells you to *look up* and she's standing on the roof, barefoot, egg-yolk yellow housedress on. When you feel panic swimming up inside you, when you feel fear throwing down an anchor in the middle of your stomach. When you climb up the tree right beside the house and onto the roof before she has a chance to jump, when you're holding her and she's shaking, when she presses up against your ear and tells you that *the angels turned into snakes and every time she hit one it split in two until the house wasn't hers anymore*. When you nod, when you tell her that *you know*, that *you're not going back into the house*, when you sit down on the back patio and call 911. When a lizard climbs up the seam of your pants and you have to flick it off. When it starts raining and it hits the cobblestones hard, splashes back up against your ankles while you're holding on to her. When you're waiting. When they take her and you work as hard as you can that winter break, work from the moment you wake up to the moment you can't stand anymore. Work to forget. Take up as many shifts as you can at the Shop-n-Save. Try to get her back. Do as many laundry loads as you can at We Will Wash You. Try to get her back. Wait all the tables they'll let you at the Denny's. Try to get her back. Work Christmas, work New Year's. Get her back, and you don't get why it works this time, but it works, and she's discharged with an assigned therapist and the chlorpromazine.

When she's better. When the angels come back only sometimes, when she tells you they're standing behind you, when the snakes are moving around your legs on Tuesdays and Wednesdays but not Mondays or Thursdays or Saturdays or Sundays. When it happens less and less and less until she's okay mostly. She's looking up at you smiling and she's okay, she's singing Al Green and she's okay mostly, dancing around the kitchen, making rice and black beans and you feel like you could cry watching her because this isn't the lady from before the angels and the snakes came but you cry because you know that this is the closest you're ever going to get. And it's okay mostly.

When senior year ends and you're still working at the laundromat and the Shop-n-Save and the diner, all those heavy stone things like *Vanderbilt* and *UPenn* and *Princeton* on your seafloor, under a million cubic tons of pressure. When you see me, sitting down in the tiny little restaurant section at the store. When you walk up to me, pain a shroud around you, an intractable prisoner inside you, that third thing your blood's made of, right along with the plasma and the cells. When you recognize me, because why wouldn't you? You pay attention to everything, always waiting for the bad to come. Looking down the street for it, sitting on the curb for it. And bad comes with me, moves through me, drives past me. I'm looking up at you. Your mom was wrong—I could never end the world with a flood again. How could I? How could I when you're drowning inside yourself? How could I when that simple fact floors me? Floors me because you were born on one of those days where the only person who could ever tread those choppy waters souls are made of is a seven-pound-six-ounce Black baby with a smile on its round little face.

You're the fire now, because you've been the water too long. And I'm gonna end the world with you."

The Oldest Sensation Is Anger

Claudette's girl shows up to Nadia's apartment with a *Simpsons* suitcase and a broken arm. It's May. She has ropey scars on her arms and the part of her chest that Nadia can see, ribbed pauses that turn her into a body stuttering. Her adoptive mother Claudette, a family friend, once drank from the river where panicked seamstresses once tossed the cocaine corrupt Haitian colonels expected them to sew into soon-to-be-exported quilts. Claudette blames the cocaine-water for the hysterectomy that hitched her to two kids (she'd wanted three), swears to this day that she can still feel poison fattening inside her. Ché is the orphan she adopted as her third.

Ché's head is shaved. Nadia can see the tiny stalks of her follicles. They're the same age—twenty—but Ché looks younger, her twenty powdered across curtainrod-collarbones and a rounder face. Here Ché is now, the first time Nadia has ever seen her in person. Around her neck she wears a choir lady's rosepink scarf, tied like an ascot.

Fiancé-killer. Nadia has heard the rumor, but it doesn't scare her like it should. All it makes her want to do is stare. Stare and stare till Ché's (maybe)killing-part would have to run out through the back of her head, tear the crown of her skull off its hinges, to escape Nadia's notice. Nadia stares at her head for so long that Ché rolls her eyes and says,

"You wanna rub it for good luck?"

Nadia reaches a hand out to do just that and Ché smacks it down. The hit makes Nadia forget that she's the taller of the two. Ché, face carefully still except for the updown updown twitch of her bottom lip as she speaks, says,

18

"Don't touch me."

"You offered."

Ché cuts her eyes at Nadia and says, with not a bit of her joking from before,

"Don't you ever touch me."

Nadia leads Ché to the back of the apartment with this new, immediate tenseness between them.

"This is the room we'll share," Nadia says, opening the door to the bedroom.

Nadia has issues with the room that she's, strangely, too embarrassed to admit to Ché. The room runs warm, the paint peels, and the latchkey middle-school kids, whose parents work until dawn hours, use the drop ladder at the base of her fire escape as monkey bars for fun on weekends. Sometimes on weekdays. Sometimes she wakes up in the middle of the night to walls melting in moonglow, catches the drywall mid-vanish while disembodied clanging and talking ring out from somewhere outside. In those moments she swears that she's caught, without her permission, waist up in the jaws of something.

"It smells musty in here," Ché says. The face she pulls makes it look like her top lip's buckled to her nose.

"Open the windows."

"And it's hot."

"Take off the goddamn scarf then."

"No," Ché just says. "Could we get a window unit in here?"

"For decoration? Sure! I'm not letting it run up the electric bill."

Ché drops her *Simpsons* suitcase against the far wall.

"The bill *you* don't pay," Ché says. It's a guess. Nadia can tell by the way Ché waits for her to respond.

The truth of it sets Nadia's teeth on edge. Nadia wishes that their exchange was as thorny as the speech between cousins—wishes it would hit soft, an ocean swell of common blood eroding its every edge (although Nadia's only guessing at the cousins thing here;

both of her parents are only children). But they're strangers slung close by all the eddying, rough, in-out-motion of Ché's life and the wax-figure stillness of Nadia's. They're strangers in the one way that Nadia realizes matters to her, as Ché turns and kneels and starts to unpack. Nadia doesn't know Ché well enough yet to tell if there's any viciousness there, anything sinister. She can't tell if Ché could've really sold a soul, made a ghost. Even though she hopes it's true. Even though Nadia wants to know if Ché has that kind of bad and where she's hiding it if so, because Nadia, for as long as she can remember, has simply—*simply*—been playing at that shit.

❧

The first time Nadia ever saw Ché was on her mother's WhatsApp.

Nadia was rolling her mother's hair into a sock bun, the fan spinning overhead like a shrunken carousel. Nadia had to use five socks because of how thick her mom's hair is—the single thing they have in common—and the toes she'd cut were scattered all over. Her mother leaned forward to pick them up, even as she chided Nadia for not doing the very same. Nadia tilted too to get a good grip, her fingers greasy with Blue Magic. Bent herself into a thirty-degree angle as her mom opened up her phone to see what Claudette had sent her. There was Ché, posed in front of a gas station with a loose, ashy tire just out of frame. Her fiancé stood next to her, a playful arm dangled around her neck like a boomerang. Ché held his elbow and rimmed herself in a return. His toothy smile was salt-white, his arm veins bulged like the seams of jeans.

The second time that Nadia saw Ché was a month ago. Facebook this time. Claudette shared a picture of Ché, taken from the side, at her fiancé's funeral. The blur of the photo gave her no mouth, so all of her feelings defected to the top half of her face. One eye smiled while the other one did a completely other thing. Darted towards the emergency exit. Twitched because an eyelash fell into it. Sang somber "Amazing Grace" in montaged English-Creole.

Claudette was not in attendance, but in her caption, she made sure to point out how distraught Ché looked, how devastated. *She has lost*. Nadia got the truth from her mother at dinner, because her mother has always hated liars and lying and lying to her children especially. Ché's fiancé died a month ago while leaving her for a Puerto Rican girl in Hialeah, after the improvised raft he'd taken from Cap-Haïtien to Miami capsized. The merchant women in Ché's town gossiped that she'd sold his soul to a demon as revenge. The rumor caught like laughter, till the chatter firmed into a broken living room window and then, when the gossipers tucked back their hunger for something more pressing, beef pâté splattered against the front door. Claudette began making arrangements for Ché's move to the States immediately. Claudette's family reputation needs time to rebound, and the bodega's needed an extra hand ever since one of their shelf stockers left.

The third time Nadia saw Ché, Claudette held up her phone as Nadia video-chatted her. This was after the funeral, when Ché finally received her visa. The conversation was stilted and awkward, half-shouted because the kids outside of Ché's window were playing soccer. When the chat ended, Claudette asked Nadia whether Ché could stay with her. Her kids and grandkids had dropped in for a week-long visit with no warning, she'd said. She couldn't possibly host Ché herself, she'd said.

Nadia didn't care. She thought of her apartment's quiet, and she said yes inside her head.

She thought of how different their lives are in heft. Nadia's mother still claims her on her taxes. Nadia lives in the apartment above her family's bodega, sleeps and breathes inside a gift. Nadia still sneaks boys into the basement of her parents' bodega and lets them eat her out between plastic-wrapped shipments of Tropiway Fufu Flour and Arizona Iced Teas, their heads wrapped in the billow of her dress like mummies. She thought of how easy it might be for Ché to need a friend—to need her so bad it made both their stomachs hurt—and she said yes out loud.

❧

The next morning, Nadia wakes up to the smell of garlic, green onion, and egg, as thick through as a stranger's visit. Nadia starts her mornings with Funyuns and watermelon juice most days. She eats and drinks from beneath the counter while she rings people up. An Asian lady once flinched when Nadia brought her arm up too quick. She stumbled back at the flash of unholstered brown. Eve once joked that Nadia's pee must feel like Sprite coming out.

Ché has her back turned when Nadia enters the kitchen. The oil in the frying pan makes it sound like there's rain choked up in the room with them. Ché's still wearing the rosepink ascot from yesterday. Wheeled around her neck, her throat its axel. Sometimes, in the bodega basement with the boys occupied between her thighs—there and good but not good enough to keep her mind all the way shut—Nadia wraps a hand around her throat and squeezes hard, a monster to herself, just to see if she has a body that could save. Even if it's distracted. Even if it's herself. The women who'd come to the hair salon she used to train at, when she was still in cosmetology school, always talked about how quickly they used to jump out of the way of motorcycle taxis in the streets of Port-au-Prince, their actions cored clear of thought like apples. Weightless and fast. Ché leans forward, a little further over the pan. Nadia can see where a patch of pink's starting to fade to white. Does Ché wear the ascot to test herself like that? Nadia waits for her to touch it, to pull. Nadia could yank, if Ché needed her to. She could.

Ché pulls bell peppers from the fridge, the ones Nadia had to dodge two yoga moms' pointy elbows to get to. She throws them into the pan, and Nadia realizes how hungry she is. Ché scoops eggs onto a large green plastic plate.

"I killed a bunch of flies with that once," Nadia says. Ché pauses. It satisfies Nadia that she now has her attention like this. Black eyes spotlighting her.

"Did you not wash the plate before you put it back? Barring that, I think I'm good."

Nadia reaches for some eggs with her spoon, and Ché tenses beside her. There's a short sizzling sound. Ché startles and curses. She's burned her good hand on the still-hot edge of the pan. Nadia can already see the spot where the skin's been pared back to bare the meat of her, the exposed flesh pink as Barbie doll lipstick. A pink so vivid you could smear it on the nearest wall. It looks painful. Nadia goes to say something, but Ché hides her hand behind her back. Ché frowns down at the eggs.

"It's not for you," Ché says.

"You used my shit to make it," Nadia says.

Ché says nothing. Nadia fixes her egg sandwich and has her breakfast.

❧

"The way you make friends," Nadia's mother once said. "It's ugly."

Nadia was twelve. She'd taken to starting rumors about the girls she wanted to be friends with, nasty things. That Gia, a funny girl whose parents used to own the laundromat across the street, had hair on her back like an Alaskan ox (you know, one of those ones you see on Animal Planet?) and her mom braids it down and dresses it up just like she does with the hair on her head; that if you hit her back you'll hear the barrettes knock against each other. That the dance team captain Lourdes could only dance so well because she'd gotten bitten by a squirrel and figured out how to steer the muscle spasms her rabies brought on. Then Nadia would sidle up to these girls, while they were crying next to the vending machines, and offer her support: *don't worry about that shit.* That was the year her mom got her a portable DVD player. She took it to school most days. She'd watch *Angus, Thongs and Perfect Snogging* with the girls while their tears dried.

The day her mother said this, said that Nadia's inside-ugly, the school had called her in from work to pick Nadia up. Here's what had happened: in the line for the girl's bathroom, Nadia idly mentioned that one of the pop show choir sopranos, asthmatic Orisa, had teeth that would never stop growing. That her buckteeth would stream and curl out of her face like skywriting. Orisa overheard. Nadia thought she was still at lunch. Orisa got so upset that her breaths came fast, then too quick, then real shallow like her lungs were lidded. She collapsed like some bridges do, gone gummy at her center then sick with gravity. Nadia reached out to catch her but she missed. Her head smashed into the linoleum, blood on blue-gray. She needed twelve stitches. Nadia got suspended for five days. Nadia told her mom,

"If I'm ugly to start off, they'll know I can't be worse."

Her mother sucked her teeth. "*Pitit, pe la.*" And Nadia knew to be quiet.

☙

"Can you still not reach it?" Eve asks.

Around five hours into an uneventful shift, one of the middle schoolers had launched a partially finished Fla-Vor-Ice popsicle onto one of the highest store shelves, the same spot they use to store excess shipments of paper towels. Besides Ché's day-long training with another employee, Angel, the day was mostly normal until then. Eve told Nadia about her fibroid for the twenty-seventh time (Nadia's been counting) while Nadia half-listened. Eve's entire life, it seems to Nadia, is a collection of good-luck crescendos hightailed

by misery. She's in her fifties now, but in her twenties and thir-
ties she was a perfume saleswoman in Jacmel while her husband
worked as the minister of tourism; even for their combined salaries,
their Rolls-Royces were suspicious. The people suspected her husband of embezzling money from the initiative that he'd set up, the
one that would train orphans who'd aged out of their homes up
into hotel workers. Folks said he stuffed the money right inside his
pants, no pockets. On his and Eve's last day in Jacmel, in Haiti at
all, the people forced him from his car and pulled his pants down
to check. They burned his car while he covered his dick with a palm
frond, while another group burned their big house too. When Eve
and her husband came to the States, they first lived in the basement
of a New York incense shop.

Nadia couldn't find the ladder. She's climbed onto the shelves,
sees a reflection of herself in the door of the freezer that holds the
frozen pizzas. The Fla-Vor-Ice is still out of reach, popsicle juice
leaking battery-blue. She can't climb onto the shelf without having
it collapse underneath her like a daytime TV stage prop.

Eve clicks her tongue, shakes her head below.

"Back in my little boutique in Jacmel, we'd have people to help
with this sort of thing."

Nadia sighs. "What are you talking about, auntie? You paid people to climb store shelves?"

"We had a ladder but the man next door was always borrowing it
to chase birds out of his mango tree. It always smelled like bird shit.
Matter fact, so did he."

Nadia feels herself laughing a bit, which is bad. Any excess movement could send her toppling.

"Auntie, pass me that broom."

Nadia grips the edge of her shelf to steady herself, uses the wide
fan of the broom brush to try and sweep the Fla-Vor-Ice to her.

"You made grown folk climb their big asses up shelves, ah? How
insulting, auntie."

Eve sucks her teeth. "Please, how silly. Most adults are not like you, not the size of my swollen thumb."

"Auntie!" Nadia hits the popsicle tube, and it slides towards the edge of the shelf, towards the pregnancy tests. She hears it splatter. She groans as she climbs down.

"What, you sent neighborhood kids up there or something?" Nadia means it as a joke, but Eve's face goes thoughtful.

"Not neighborhood kids. The ones who lived with us. Helped clean and cook and such. And we didn't have to pay them, they were like family."

"Didn't pay them? At all?" Nadia has heard of the restaveks, the child servants, but she'd always assumed they got something for their service besides the dubious hospitality. *Some*thing. "It didn't have to be paper money. Not even candies?" Nadia's voice is still light, but the set of Eve's jaw makes her feel like she's misspoken.

"They were like family," Eve says again.

Orisa's family had a kid like that, Nadia remembers. The kid lived with them. Orisa came to the States at eleven, damp with story. Ready to share. She told them about her family's three-story on the beach, how meat tastes honest on the island (the meat here tastes like it's hiding the best of itself), how she had a friend who could walk on anything barefoot (broken Heineken bottles, the thrown-away rims of cars, a dismembered mule hoof once). That her friend had no parents. They lived with her ("It was like a forever-sleepover!" Orisa said), set out Orisa's uniforms for the day before they both went off to school. At lunch one day, Orisa told them about how her friend would sometimes be pulled away from their soccer games so they could wipe down tables in the house, wash dishes, do laundry. Nadia has lived her whole life with choices. Choices sugar her gums. At cosmetology school, she used to twist the locs of their hair models so tight that they'd jerked away from her. The fourth time it happened, she just walked out of the practice salon. She let the silence and distance quit for her. She still has the salon apron she'd left in.

But Nadia's older now, knows better. After she hears this from Eve, she can hardly look at her for the rest of the shift. Nadia's eyes go everywhere like shrapnel: ding the cameras, nearly slash through the menthol boxes behind her, nearly slash through the lotto tickets.

One of the stalls in the bathroom, the one closest to the window, has a broken door. Later that day, when Nadia goes in to wash her hands of a spilled slushie, the broken door drags open a bit. Nadia is about to rush out, to give whoever it is their privacy, when she notices the shaved head and blue arm cast.

Ché can't see her yet. Nadia watches in the mirror. Ché sits on the closed lid of the toilet. She holds her burnt hand up to her face, the back of it still pink. She moves her broken arm so that her dangling fingers touch the open wound. She slides it up the back of her hand, to where unmarred brown skin lazes intact. Then she rubs down from the brown to the pink again. Her skin streaks like dough. She does it again, then again, till she's pulled brown right over the exposed pink. Her hand looks brand new.

Nadia swallows, her head shocked, buzzing like a Deep South summer wadded up with mosquitoes. She looks away before Ché can catch her staring. When she leaves the bathroom and reenters the store, somebody's toddler has knocked over a glass jar full of cashews.

The apartment seems empty when Nadia gets back in the evening. The pan Ché used for eggs this morning sits unwashed in the sink, the plastic green plate right over it. Nadia thinks that this is not at all how a guest should behave, broken arm or not. If Ché is able to cook with her broken arm, she should be able to wash the pan she used. Nadia's pettiness drives her to walk right past it. There are broken eggshells on the ground near the trash can, where Ché seems to have missed. Nadia feels her irritation growing, but when she spots Ché in the living room her head clogs up with questions, and she asks,

"Are you still mad at your fiancé for leaving?"

Ché walks over to the fridge and opens it with her good hand. Nadia stares at it so hard Ché should be able to feel her gaze clamping down on it.

"That subtlety's unmatched. You should be a fucking diplomat."

Nadia's face gets hot and Ché looks back at her, smiles a bit. She curses in English like it doesn't count, her fluency just a visit.

"Don't know if I'm allowed to be mad at somebody who's dead."

"I don't think it works like that."

"Oh? And how many dudes have died on you?"

"I said 'I don't *think*.'"

Ché leans against the fridge and watches her. The ascot is a necklace around her throat. It's new and still has its tag. She stands there hooped in a beginning. Nadia feels like she's been living in a midpoint since she dropped out of cosmetology school, no start, no end. She has the sudden urge to unknot the ascot and tie it around both of their necks, manacle them together like flower stems, turn them into a bouquet of eyelashes and teeth. Ché says,

"And if I told you that I wanted to do the two-step on his grave, smoke a joint on it, eat takeout on it, spit soda onto it, what then?"

"You can dance?"

Ché laughs.

"Ask me what you wanna ask me."

"What?" But Nadia knows.

"Did I go to the bokor. Did I sell Raoul out because he wanted other pussy. Did I cut myself and drain my blood into a soup pot for the deal. Is that why I look so scraped up." These don't feel like questions.

When Ché brings up her scars they're all Nadia can see for several seconds. A scattered blossoming—all along her sternum, under an eye, right under her hairline—ridges ready to bear bone-fruit. Marrow-ripe. If Nadia hit her hard enough, she thinks Ché would gem the walls with new milk.

Ché watches herself be watched. Then she says,

"I drove motorcycle taxis in Léogâne."

Nadia's seen the motorcycle taxis, but only in grainy Android videos that her mom and Claudette show her. Nadia looks at Ché and sees her as she might have been: threading through overstuffed camionnettes, the thighs of strangers parenthesizing her hips.

Nadia can see the back of her hand much more clearly when she's up close like this. It's definitely healed, but not all the way. The new skin is just a bit lighter than the rest of Ché's hand.

"Did you like it?" Nadia asks.

Ché laughs again. "Yeah. It could've killed me."

Nadia met him twenty minutes ago. She was still sorting through her irritation from that morning, when Ché had made breakfast (French toast this time) and dropped another one of her pans into the sink without washing it, right on top of the one from yesterday. He came in looking for mop pads for his Swiffer, dressed in his Cinemark attendant uniform. She told him *we don't carry that* and he asked *can you check, please please* and she knows that desperation when it's inside you for any reason at all harasses everything else into its color so she told him to follow her into the back and now she's laying on a stack of long-grain rice bags with his head beneath her skirt.

His long nails bite into the meat of her hip. She's solid, congealed. More than any salt-white toothed, other-pussy-wanting ghost, less than Ché. Ché, who must have another body coiled up inside her, must have some place she's pulling more of herself from. Nadia wants that. No, more than that. More bodies than that. She'd like to matter that wildly, matter everywhere and all at once. She's suddenly hoping that some of her has condensed inside every person she's ever done this with, prays for multiple bodies. Versions of her bunched up behind the corks of their navels. She'd come out of their abdomens, skin of their bellies hiked up like skirts to release her. There, there, there.

"I'm there," she groans into the quiet, and the nails cut her deeper.

Her eyes are bleary when they open. But there's still enough light to see the top of the Cinemark's head by, and through this dark sheer as mesh she sees Ché standing at the door Nadia had chosen not to close. Wants Ché to see her Bad, her here. Trust me, trust me. Ché blinks slowly, like a cat might. When she backs away and leaves, the Cinemark attendant is still catching his breath.

॰

"Oh, look at you! And when did this one happen?" Claudette tilts Ché's head to the side to get a better look at a healed cut on her temple. Ché looks like she's gritting her teeth against a flinch.

Claudette always stops by on Thursdays, in her scrubs and on her way to the hospital, to buy one of those iced coffees Nadia is sure only high school sophomores and adult sociopaths drink. This Thursday is no exception, even though it seems to Nadia that nothing should matter today but what happened in the storeroom yesterday. Nothing should matter but that Ché knows what Nadia is capable of.

"My love, I keep telling you to stay off of those motos. It's not suitable . . ." Claudette pats Ché's cheek, and Nadia recognizes it as the unspoken second half of her sentence: . . . *for a face that looks like this.* Ché favors Grace Jones, looks so much like the close-up photos Nadia has seen of her in vintage *Essence* magazines, beauty a spectacle.

"Yes ma'am," Ché says, voice a little strained as Claudette tips her head back to check beneath her chin.

"And you're eating, right? Cooking for Nadia too?"

"Yes ma'am—"

Claudette turns to Nadia. "Nadia, how's her cooking?"

Nadia fumbles the pen she was playing with. Ché watches her over Claudette's shoulder as they both wait for her answer. Ché wiggles the fingers of her casted arm. Nadia wonders for the first time since she saw her fix her own burn why Ché hasn't done the same for her bone.

"It's great, auntie. I'd pay money for it."

Claudette laughs, delighted. She turns back and pats Ché's shoulder.

"I'll come by again soon, okay? Be a good guest."

Ché's eyes are still on Nadia as Claudette leaves. She's wearing the barest bit of a smile.

"You gonna start paying me for my cooking now?"

"You gonna start replacing the shit you use?"

Eve's just finished counting the boxes of Little Debbie brownies the delivery man dropped off near the entrance. She straightens up, looks to Ché, and asks,

"You drove motos?"

"Sure did, auntie. I could drive a moto through a Christmas wreath."

Eve sucks her teeth at the overfamiliarity, and Ché looks delighted by her irritation. Eve says,

"We should get rid of those cursed things. My nephew lost a leg at an intersection in Aux Cayes. Can't even wash his own ass now, the poor thing. It's a good thing he got married while he was still whole, has somebody who's stuck with him."

"Eve," Nadia says, face hot with offense.

"What?" Eve says. She nods at Ché's immobilized arm. "Look at her."

"War prize, auntie," Ché says, lifting the arm towards Eve.

Eve rolls her eyes. She continues. "And losing a leg? That's lucky. The mountain pass from Jean-Rabel to La Pointe? Six motos fell off the edge last month, passengers and all. They found them with their necks snapped. One's head was completely gone."

Nadia swallows against her bile. Ché has gone back to her work, stacking baked beans from a huge red carton. She moves so so stiffly, like the stillness will make her injuries, the ones Nadia can't stop counting off now, wane completely out of sight. The bells chime over the store doors. Angel comes in with a long wide white box.

"Krispy Kreme was giving out free donuts," he says. His grin is wide.

༜

The middle schoolers have a new game. They'll climb onto the highest spots they can find in the alley—the trashcan, the fire-escape ladder. A crowd of them will stand before the climber and, when the kid high above them launches themselves from their spot, they'll try to move out of the way in time to avoid the crash of flesh. But the whole point, it seems to Nadia, is that the climber-turned-jumper wants the crash.

She sees them playing through her bathroom window as she's brushing her teeth. The late-night security guard for the building across the alley chases them out as she's wiping her mouth. The kids laugh and shriek as they run away.

༜

By the next day, Ché has used all three of Nadia's pans. She leaves them untouched in the sink and Nadia still feels her pettiness packing itself above and below and around all her vitals. She thinks it would feel the same if somebody punched a folding fan between her ribs and opened it. The eggs from the first day crust, and French toast from the second day circuits the edges of the second pan. With the third pan, Ché makes bacon so succulent it is all Nadia thinks about for the rest of the day. The third pan sits on top of the other two, bits of leftover bacon clinging to its white like moles on a face. Old grease clogs the air and turns their lungs to vats for frying. Nadia thinks she could inhale a whole raw fish and breathe it out cooked all the way through.

A few days later, Nadia wakes up to get a glass of water. The fluorescent light from the bathroom comes down onto the hardwood like a dropped white towel. Another unlocked door, Ché behind it.

Nadia inches towards the door and peers inside.

Ché is washing her face. Both of her hands scrub at her cheeks, her eyes closed like she's found a way to dream on her feet. The blue cast sits next to her on the sink, cracked open on one side.

She means to confront Ché that morning, but Claudette comes to the apartment early and takes Ché out. It's the weekend and they both have the day off. Nadia walks around the apartment sweating anger, her face and arms hot to touch. Ché is gone for hours. When Nadia hears the duplicate of her own key turning in the lock, the one her mother drove her to AutoZone to make, Nadia goes to the kitchen to stand next to the sink. She listens as Ché slips off her shoes near the door. Ché comes into view, a Macy's bag hanging off her arm. Nadia says,

"Wash this shit." A roach tap-dances across one faucet handle and Nadia stops herself from shuddering. Nadia knows she should be irritated by Ché's lying, and scared, and she is both—irritated and a bit scared—but more than both those things, she finds herself excited. Here is Ché, a liar. Even her skin lies. A liar through-and-through, her Bad somewhere Nadia can see. She wants to see more of Ché's Bad.

Ché wiggles the fingers of her casted arm at Nadia.

"I saw you," Nadia says.

"Saw me what?"

"In the bathroom."

Ché's face goes tense for a quarter second, then it's back to normal. Back to what it always looks like, like she's on the verge of a smile.

"Spying on me through a gap in the bathroom stall . . . Your bodega doesn't have an HR department, does it?"

"Your arm isn't broken."

"Ma'am said you dropped out of a cosmetology program, not med school."

"It's not broken. Wash the dishes." Nadia feels her anger mounting.

"You looked at anatomy books between scalping people with your plier-fingers?"

Nadia's breath catches a bit. She'd specifically asked her mother not to tell people why she'd left school—that she had no exciting reason except that she wasn't very good at it. The simple honest truth of it hurts more. She used to tell people that she'd been expelled for selling their good practice wigs on eBay. Her mother must've told Claudette everything.

For a moment, all Nadia can see is the cast. A flashing blue light. It belongs at a rave. Anger cramps her stomach, ugly as acid. And the excitement, too. The excitement, most of all. She marches over. She grabs Ché's arm, pulls at it to try and rip the cast off. The material under her fingers is rough and gridded like burlap. Ché's black eyes spotlight her again as she grabs at Nadia's throat, her cheek, her hair, scratches at the fleshiest part of her nose, gets her above the eyebrow, fingers in her mouth now (Nadia tastes plastic, probably from the Macy's bag), and Nadia's trying to wrench Ché's arm so it'll hurt (see, see? Here's the lie. Here's your Bad. Show me. Show me). For a long, wide moment, they're pressed into each other, a single tilt as they fall to the ground. Freight trains running through the night aren't louder than their breathing. Ché scratches her temple, and Nadia feels it smarting. When Nadia bites Ché's fingers, Ché flinches like she had when she'd burned herself. Ché lets go, pulls her arm out of Nadia's grasp while Nadia's distracted. Does it quick, with grace. One single heave.

Ché stands up, panting. Nadia's still on the ground. Ché looks like she wants to slap Nadia hard, turn her mouth into a coin purse rattling with molars. Her chest rises and falls with the anger.

"Don't you ever touch me," she says.

But Nadia, on her back on the ground, thinks that there isn't room enough in English or Creole for whatever Ché actually means. For how whatever she actually means wants to swell itself big. Nadia should have a *sorry* in her somewhere for Ché, but what she does say is,

"I saw you. In the storeroom. When I went down there with the…"

Ché's anger is still there, no doubt, but as she stands over Nadia it fissures to let something milder through. Nadia hesitates to call it humor. Ché says,

"Saw you too. Seems like you do that kind of thing a lot."

That's what makes Nadia sit up, frowning. "Are you shaming me?"

"No. It's just that you do all this wild shit … well, shit *you* think is wild, because you feel safe. Bungee jumping when I *swear*, I bet *anything*, your ass couldn't skydive."

Nadia can't help her defensiveness. "And you could?"

Ché shrugs. "I have. I've had to. My wild has a reason to it. My wild saves me. Always."

Nadia cannot get to sleep that night, and finds herself jealous of the still, quiet form she takes to be Ché on the floor beside her bed. The kids are loud, louder than usual. She wishes there were a poltergeist in the alley, wishes that it would scoop up garbage hot from the can and pelt them with it so they'd leave.

There's the panicked, "Oh shit, guard's coming!" then a single loud groan packed up with pain. Then there's silence.

The drop from noise to quiet is steep, not even eased along by the appearance of the building security guard. First there's fullness, trunks of noise, then there's nothing. Nadia gets up. She heads for the window in her bathroom. When she peers down, she sees two forms. One is a middle schooler, stick-thin, laying on his back. He's gripping his leg, his face pinched 'cause it hurts so bad. The other, with a rosepink ascot around their neck, is unmistakably Ché. The ascot is loose, mostly askew. Ché must've just thrown it on and ran down. There is a ropey line across her neck, the longest scar Nadia's seen on her by far.

The boy's face is gray, and his eyes are shut tight. Nadia wonders if he even knows Ché is there with him. Ché digs her fingers into the edge of her cast and cracks it open. Then she grips the boy's leg. Nadia can see where the bone is shoving up against the skin, impending. Ché tightens her hold, right over the bulge of bone. The kid should be screaming, but he's not. His face is loosening. Ché keeps opening and closing her hand, like she's squeezing dishwater out of a sponge. Open, shut, open shut. When she takes away her hand, the boy's leg is as straight as it must have been before. He still looks disoriented, but his color has returned.

Nadia's face is all but pressed up against the window glass. She has brief mental flashes of snapping her own leg bone, an arm, a rib maybe, to see what Ché could do with her. To see, just to see.

❦

The next day brings sweat with it. Ché uses a pot to make breakfast—oatmeal—because the pans are still unclean. Two roaches butt heads on the faucet. Sunheat hits the asphalt outside the bodega and trampolines towards its sky. Reeds of it prong upright like the bristles of a hairbrush. The sidewalk's so hot that when Nadia goes outside to sign off on a new shipment of Pedialyte she feels the baking cement through the thin soles of her tennis shoes. She feels like she's doing barefoot penance across a running car engine. The earth is pregnant with the hottest June. The delivery man has to wipe his sweaty palm against his pant leg before he lends her his pen.

Nadia picks up the box. As a strain hoards itself in Nadia's neck and shoulders, Ché stands beside the entrance. She lifts her cast meaningfully and asks,

"You wanna try harder this time?" The sweat on Ché's temples and nose makes her look laminated.

Nadia recognizes this for the taunt that it is. But it's full of much kinder things, much less thorny than that first day. Nadia even smiles at her as she waddles inside the store with the box. Someone small streaks past her calf and she nearly trips.

"Jonas!"

It's Claudette's voice. Nadia's still steadying herself as she watches Claudette's grandson (Nadia thinks he's about five now) rush into the store.

"Sorry about that, Nadia," Claudette says.

She pats Nadia's shoulder, nearly tips her over with the casual force. Claudette turns to Ché.

"How is your arm, my love?"

Nadia's arms ache terribly as she walks through the propped-open door. Ché, Claudette, and their conversation trail her.

"The pain is mostly gone, ma'am."

Nadia stumbles to the dairy section where she can finally set the box down. Angel is wiping down the heat-sticky counter for the third or fourth time that day, covering for Eve, who's at a doctor's appointment for her latest fibroid.

"That's good! You'll be able to help around here in no time."

". . . Right, ma'am."

Jonas speeds past Nadia again. He slingshots his hard little knee right into her calf. She winces while he disappears around the corner. He's arcing his *Scooby Doo* plushie through the air like it's an airplane.

"Jonas!" Claudette shouts again. She says to Ché,

"I'll get you a sling to strap your arm to your chest. We can't have it swinging around like a graduation tassel."

"And I'll pay for it myself, ma'am."

"Hm? With your moto money?" Her tone gets a bit tighter. It's the first time Nadia has heard her speak to Ché with anything less than fondness. "Keep it in case you run out of Kotex or shoelaces. You don't need it for anything bigger than that."

Nadia walks around the corner. She can see Claudette and Ché's faces. She swallows at the moment's strange stress, against the sense that she is missing important things here. She's seeing their shared lives in snatches, she thinks, observing a hand that's missing some fingers.

"Ma'am, I just think that—"

"Ché, don't—"

The thin metal of a merchandising shelf smacks loud against the linoleum. Claudette and Ché are interrupted. Nadia can't help her recoil at the sound. A few steps in front of her, the shelf of chips has been knocked over. Doritos and Lays and Fritos blotch the ground in their reds and yellows and manufactured oranges. Jonas stands beside it all, his *Scooby Doo* plushie now lowered, his eyes as wide and as shocked as they'd be if he'd just watched someone else tip over the display.

Claudette hurries over and grabs his arm.

"Boy, what did I say? What did I *say*?"

Claudette looks like she's lost all of the meat in her face. Her cheekbones become clumps of balled concrete. Ché watches with a clenched jaw. Discomfort tubes Nadia's stomach into a roll of pennies, even before Claudette raises a hand to hit Jonas on his back.

Once, and Ché jolts like it is her. Then again. Ché jolts. Then not again, because Nadia is speed-walking forward, her stomach a pinwheel now. Jonas is crying.

"Auntie!" Nadia says. Claudette looks up, her face still meatless. She smiles but it has nowhere to settle. Her hand tightens around Jonas's arm.

"Apologize to Nadia," she says.

Jonas sniffles. "S . . . so—"

Nadia doesn't let him finish. She thinks her pinwheel-stomach will cycle straight through her viscera if she does.

"It's okay, Jonas," she says. She looks up at Claudette, holds her gaze even though she doesn't want to. "Auntie, it's okay. I'll clean this up no problem."

Nadia looks up at Ché too, who's looking away from her. She walks towards the back of the bodega, towards the cases of vanilla Sport Shake, as Nadia dabs at Jonas's damp face with the bottom of her shirt.

～

Nadia returns to the apartment later that day. Three roaches now. She tries to wash the dishes but she can't. It's not a pettiness that stops her now but Ché, in her mind, looking away. Hit by Claudette through Jonas by Claudette through Jonas by Claudette. How many times had she . . . Ché, Nadia means. How many times had she . . .

Nadia waits for Ché to get back, to finish taking inventory with Angel. When Ché does get home, all Nadia can say is,

"You call her ma'am."

"Yeah."

"Not mom."

"Mom's dead."

"But—"

"Dead."

"Your arm's not broken."

Ché sits on the arm of the sofa. Then she says,

"It was." It's quiet for a bit before she speaks again.

"Do you know how long a broken bone takes to heal? It broke clean through just this month. Doctors saw it. Ma'am has pictures on her phone. Things would look strange if everybody knew I was okay."

Nadia's heart beats hard inside her chest. "This month?"

"Yeah," Ché says. Her eyes are black crows in the sky of her face. "I crashed. Eve's right. Jean-Rabel to La Pointe, it's a shitty route."

Nadia's Creole is not as good as Ché's English, but she swallows and tries anyway. She repeats,

"Jean-Rabel to La Pointe?"

"Yeah."

Ché slides down onto a couch cushion, properly sitting now. She reaches out for Nadia's face. Nadia's reminded of the scratch on her cheek from their fight. It was never bleeding or anything, even at its worst, but it's unmistakable. Ché presses a thumb beside the scratch, where the skin is still unmarked, and swipes across the expanse of the scratch once. Hard. Nadia's foot jerks with the sudden pain. Ché pulls away, and Nadia touches her face. No scratch.

Ché frowns for a moment, like she's struggling with something. Then she says,

"I didn't just break my arm."

Nadia doesn't say a thing. She's afraid that something in her voice, in her words, will make Ché change her mind. Shutter herself. She sits so still that you could break a wave against her.

"The harder I get hit, the more time it takes to fix it. This, what I'm about to show you, is from two months ago."

Ché reaches for the ascot around her neck, her eyes still on Nadia. She unknots it. Nadia sees the long scar again, waxy, ridged. Then the bandana's off completely.

"Don't scream," Ché warns.

Ché rolls up the ascot and pushes it against Nadia's mouth until she opens up and holds it between her teeth like a bit.

Ché sits up straight. She grips her own chin and tips her head back. Further back, then further back still. Her neck splits along the scar like it's a perforated edge. No blood spurts. The veins, intact, stretch easy like gummy noodles. There is salmon-pink meat and the cane of her throat, rippling. Ché is ajar. Nadia wants to scream, but not from fear. She chews the rosepink ascot and she watches.

Sylpha

Before Sylpha had any children, she'd wanted, more than anything, to train her dreams. All the Haitian women she knew had had dreams of the number of children they'd have before they existed in the world, and what kind of people they'd be, and Sylpha started to think that the dreaming was the point. The dreaming made a funnel of itself and forced real life to drip right through, forced real life, molten, to run here or there. And if she could train her dreams, she could control the pour of reality through them.

So before she had any children, almost every day after dinner and before bed, Sylpha would sit on the edge of her comforter and breathe deep for two minutes straight. She towed the air in through her mouth and hooked her lips closed so it would have nowhere to go. She expected that it might bulge under her skin, that she'd look like she'd been set to a boil until the new free space inside her met the new free space inside her and she grew so big she tore through the roof, the house tight around her waist.

Because then she'd be big enough to pick her dreams up by the scruffs of their necks, those big wild things that won't stop snarling and scratching and splitting off and growing in every direction until you get so tired of tracking their limbs that you figure it's easier to just wake up.

It's a Haitian thing. If something big is gonna happen to you or someone close to you, good or bad, you'll feel it even when you're closed shut, asleep. If it's big it'll be clumsy. You won't need your eyes or your ears to know it's coming. Your dreams will give you hints about it. Sylpha's great-aunt Fiona has three sets of twins, and she'd told Sylpha that before she found out she was pregnant with each pair, she'd dreamt of two yuca roots as thick around as her head. And in those dreams Fiona found herself clinging to the walls of a house with no floor, used nails as sharp as talons to cut into the hard cement and to climb across into the first room nearby. It would always be a bathroom, and the two roots would always be on the counter, so big they curled into the sink bowl, one on top of the other.

And Sylpha's wanted twins ever since she first realized that that's what her cousins are. The thought that your body had made two of something just because it could . . . there was something cocky and beautiful and ridiculous about it that had Sylpha looking at each set of Fiona's twins, even when she was little and much younger than any of them, with the sleepless intensity of somebody who wanted something so bad they'd taken to waking up in the middle of the night to see if they'd gotten it yet.

So she used to train her dreams. She tried to force it. Whenever they'd finished having sex and they'd taken their shower, Arlo would try to stay up with her, let her cord together her love for Sade and her "obsession" (that's what Arlo loved to call it, but he was wrong. He was! She only watched it whenever it came on because she liked to critique it) with *Voyager* in explanations that only made sense to her. But he never could. So she'd get some time to sit there and make herself big before she slept so she could grab her dreams by the backs of their necks and make them take her to the house with no floor.

But when Cari comes she comes alone. They tell Sylpha to try to get some sleep, right after the birth. Cari has a full head of hair and these pretty beauty marks that stumble across her marble-round face like it's accidental. Sylpha thinks of black seeds spilled across a cherry wood tabletop. Sylpha lays on her side and stares at her daughter all night, sleeping small inside her hard plastic case. The door's shut up so tight the light from the hallway can't squirm even a single finger through the space between the hinges or the spot between the sill and floor. The only flashes that stumble into the room to interrupt the dark come from the moon. They scatter across the linoleum between her bed and her daughter's crib-like quarters. It's like Sylpha can hear them. The baby hears them too and she wakes up to cry.

When Sylpha holds her she is heavy in her arms though she weighs nothing, and Sylpha realizes that it must be her, not the baby, because her blood's too stiff. It feels like what she feels when she looks at Arlo or her cousins, like love but hardened over. Is it ever supposed to feel like this? She's so dense she knows if she moves around too much she'll fall through the second floor and take the whole hospital with her. There's no way she can hold love like this for more than one thing at a time but it's like she can't help it, she can't help but wonder what would have happened if Cari had a twin. If she'd made another person for her. This thing, this wanting with no getting, is a sweet, titled failure.

Manticore

When my sister calls me, I am on my knees with an arm under the canopied princess bed of my youngest.

There is a coin-slot darkness below the box spring, and my youngest Yani fears herself small enough to tumble into it. She tells me that when (not "if") she slips, she will be locked in from the outside. She does not fear for me, she says, because "manmi's hips are too wide for her to fit completely."

I have time for things like this now. The steel plant for which I used to work as a research analyst was built too close to the Everglades. Almost a month ago, with the offices empty for President's Day, the bottom half of the building sank into the swamp. For years, my coworkers and I were suspended over an earth too tender to hold us and no one cared until it was too late. We've been sent home for a couple of months while they rebuild somewhere drier.

When my sister calls me and I pick up, my hand has just closed around what Yani recruited me to search for—Punk Rock Barbie's rubbery head. I'm so happy that I've found it that I sound giddy when I answer,

"Ella?"

"Taya? You'd better come over here and grab Kiki before Mrs. Powell does."

It's midafternoon, maybe an hour and a half after the high school lets out. Kiki, my oldest, should be at the weather channel assistantship Elijah pulled weight to get her. The one we'd decided might keep her out of trouble. We've known for a while that Kiki's is not a quiet recklessness. Not the one that drives the kids downtown to

45

drink their vodka out of Capri Sun pouches outside the CVS. It's the refusal to accept her body as an easily destructible element. She crosses streets without looking and she doesn't cover her mouth and nose when I ask her to bleach the tub unless I tell her to.

And she jumps off of things. Seven months ago, while she thumbed her broken ankle on a disordered hospital bed, Elijah and I met gazes over her braided head and decided with our eyes that we had to come up with a longform distraction, the assistantship. We would do what the child psychologists could not. This daring would not pass like baby teeth, as we thought once.

"Mrs. Powell?" My good mood is gone. "What happened?"

My sister tells me that Kiki was hanging around outside of the Dave & Buster's with some classmates. That Kiki joined in on the collective post-school habit of the teenagers around here, the one where they'll linger just outside of the D&B like spilt honey on marble, conscious of the "must be eighteen-plus for entry" rule as only those cramped inside those last few pre-eighteen years can be. My sister asks me if I know those huge, multicolored concrete spheres that line the entrance, the ones that kind of look like gum balls? and I say yes.

Ella says that Kiki climbed onto one of them, then began to jump from concrete sphere to concrete sphere as her classmates laughed and yelled and rolled their eyes and wondered out loud, "are you out of your damn mind?" Ella admits that the hops were so smooth that for a minute, even she and her new Trinidadian man (the one with three gold dental crowns, not the one with his own line of braiding hair) were impressed. Kiki cleared those few feet like she was videogame-controlled. My sister realized that it was her niece after just a few more jumps, but before she could yell out, "Get down from there Anaïca!" Kiki lost her footing.

Mrs. Powell's boy Arley (you know, the pole vaulter?) was standing a bit too close to the last blue sphere, and Kiki fell on him. When she rolled off, he was screaming and clutching at his knee, and my sister told her Trinidadian man to start the car while she ran over to grab Kiki. My sister took Kiki to her own house instead of mine since the D&B is just a few blocks away from her and Mrs. Powell lives just a few houses away from me.

Ella says that Mrs. Powell has already made a Facebook status about what happened. When I put her on speakerphone to check the post, I find that it is a solid, nearly impenetrable block of text.

It begins with seven exclamation points and includes her son's full government name, *Arley James Gabriel McNielson-Powell*, and moves on to announce that her son has torn his ACL, that even though they have yet to see the doctor she just *knows* that he has, because a mother just knows these things, and did you know that when he was a baby he would kick at her kidney like a Brazilian soccer player and that's how she knew he was going to be an athlete and what is he going to do now because when an athlete tears their ACL one time the likelihood that they will tear it again increases, it's just like untended water damage to a roof, and that little bug-eyed girl has no home-training and there's only so much that a poor woman with a fibroid can do so she will leave this situation in the hands of the All Mighty (mostly).

"The woman works quicker than a bad rash," Ella says.

"Is Kiki okay?"

"Isn't she always?"

"Ella."

"Yes."

I get off the phone and reattach the Barbie doll's head to her hard plastic neck. I hand Yani a body intact, make sure she's somewhere my husband can watch her before I leave for Kiki.

I'm more relieved than I think I should be that Elijah managed to find Kiki an internship at the station where he's head anchor.

I have been trying to summon my grandfather's spirit for advice since the first time Kiki was suspended for jumping off of swings at recess when she was little—even set up my own makeshift Vodou altar in one of our back rooms—and I have yet to reach him. His wisdom bent to fit Ella and me no matter how big we got, handled our "where do the gummies go when we eat them?" just as well as our "would we really burn if we walked into the Catholic church on Biscayne?" The cockiest part of me sees Elijah's solution as a stopover, just until I can get my Granpa to hear me.

Ella went with me to the bodega on Flagler last time to replace the Florida water and summoning rattles. The Florida water must cleanse the room that the spirit enters, and the rattles are prosthetic throats, made to help our chanting. Every summoning needs both. These are the technicalities that I repeat to myself each time I fail, the knowledge a comfort.

Ella and I were knotted at our joints as kids, inseparable, before our grandfather died and the mourning cleaved us. These trips are how we relearn each other.

The man who rang us up asked us if we wanted to come to the ceremony that he and his cousin were holding near Wynwood. Ella said "no" quicker than I could, like she'd stolen my tongue. While I waited in the car, she ran back in because she had to pee. I pretended not to notice her through the store glass, buying her own Florida water. This is the poorest kept secret between us. That we're trying, on our own, to reach him. I wonder if what keeps Ella from asking me for help is embarrassment, because she used to run so hard from this. I'm not sure what's stopping me.

When I got home I tried again. Kneeled in the back room with the full bowl and the candles burning. My grandfather used to say that the spirit of my grandmother would appear to him in the form of an ewe, but that she would speak in a voice that was her own. I waited to see what form he would take for me.

I always lock the door, but it is not to keep out my children. Kiki is a child who feels guilt easily, hasn't asked about this room since the incident that nearly got her expelled from school, and Yani associates the "back" of anything with darkness. I bolt the door to keep Elijah out. He grew up in a family where, when their people die, they burn their pictures and shoes to cauterize the living souls of those they leave behind. My husband believes that the past can make you sick if you're not careful. We're so in sync on most things, but this is what we don't talk about because it might cave our accord. I pretend not to hear him breathing right outside the door, the whole of him a single bloated lung. Ridiculous. If I was actually communing with some foul thing, what could he do to pull me back?

Elijah calls me while I'm at a red light, four blocks away. Next to the horse trail where I'd chaperoned one of Kiki's school trips, the one that nearly got her expelled by the administrators. We are now banned from the trail.

"Eli?"

"Mrs. Powell's outside."

"What?" The car jerks forward with me as I try to figure out how to be in two places at once.

"Don't worry, Ta. I'll call Sister Roseline." Though I do not like her, and I'm sure she only speaks to Elijah to fish for gossip, it was Sister Roseline who'd stood up for us at the PTA meeting ten years ago. She is also the only person Mrs. Powell listens to. Kiki had brought in one of the sacred rattles from my back-room altar for show-and-tell and announced to her class that her grandfather was tucked inside it. This was months after the swing set issue. The other kids were restless with nightmares of their own grandparents shoved up inside small, portable places. One little girl smashed the lightbulb in her bedside lamp and needed three stitches. Mrs.

Powell, whose own Arley took to poking eggs with toothpicks to see if his grandmother would dribble out, tried to get Kiki expelled for inciting panic. Sister Roseline rolled her eyes then. "Come on, Jasmine, she's a six-year-old."

"Okay," I say. "How's Yani?"

"Relax, Ta. She has a daddy too."

～

The door is unlatched when I arrive at my sister's house. It is a routine of hers that nothing can break her out of, as much as it makes me nervous.

I wonder whether she'd be more careful if she didn't have the credit of an insomniac gambler and could buy the house. Could make it hers. Could own it like she's tried to own other things. A year out of college, when they tore down my Granpa's old house, Ella took a 23andMe test that worked parts of her loose and gave her a segmented breakdown of what we are. Sixty-six percent East African, from Burundi. I was there, spending winter break with my left arm wedged between her couch cushions. I watched her fold herself over the edge of the tiny bathroom's sink. She spit into the test tube. I wanted to rush over and cinch her lips closed like I used to when we were little and she'd eat graham crackers with her mouth open. When the results came in, she signed up for one of those mail-in credit card offers and went to Gitega. I remember the day she left because it was the anniversary of our grandfather's death and she could not go to the cemetery with me because of her trip.

I've always tried harder than she has to remember our life in Brickell. I attended every single Caribbean carnival in downtown Miami dressed in the sequined bikini and the gigantic angel's wings, even though the sight of my body even a little nude makes my eyes water, and even though I'd leave an hour in.

"He would be angry with you for doing this," I said when she told me about Gitega and her plans to leave me alone for months. I hoped it would wound her into staying.

She rolled her eyes and it made me feel like she was the older one. "I'll bring you something."

When I come into the rented house, Ella is making tea and Kiki is doing her homework at the table. It's like nothing strange has happened, or is happening, or ever will. That's the thing with my blood. We cork our disasters and revisit them when they're colder. Anything can be put off.

I walk over to Kiki's table and take her face in my hands, check for marks. My Granpa thought that pain carries in the face, racked up under brow ridges. I used to think it was ridiculous. Now I tilt Kiki's head from side to side, hoping that if there's pain somewhere it will lump where I can feel it immediately.

"Manmi," she says. I back off, ignoring Ella's amused little smile in my periphery.

"Why weren't you at the station?" I ask her.

"They don't actually need me there."

"Yes, they do. You make sun cutouts for the four o'clock puppet show."

"Manmi."

"Okay, let's try this: what were you doing jumping around like you lost your good sense? Haven't you learned anything?"

I tried to enroll her in track once, after the child psychologists did nothing. I don't know what else to say except that she was terrible at it. At her first meet, she knocked down every single hurdle.

My phone chimes with a message from Elijah. It's a photo of Mrs. Powell in her Isuzu Trooper, idling curbside, centimeters from our property. Elijah has captured her in the middle of fixing her wig in her rearview mirror. His text reads that there's been an accident on Flagler, and Sister Roseline will be delayed. He asks me if I think he should go outside instead to talk to her. I consider the grade of irritation I'd reach if Kiki was in Arley's position, measure it up against the fact that Mrs. Powell once sprayed sunscreen into her ex-husband's eye after he called Arley an idiot; I was the one who, passing by their porch on my jog, called an ambulance. Likely another point against me in her book. I text back *no*.

I look up to Kiki trying to slink away into the living room.

"Anaïca," I say.

She sits back down and answers my question. "I wanted to see if I was all healed up from the accident."

"That's what the physical therapy's for."

"I walk through parallel bars for two hours. That doesn't prove anything."

"It's safer." I give her a hard look so that my meaning's clear. She looks half-embarrassed. Elijah says that I'm the only person who can make Kiki feel shame. He said it like it was some sort of marvel. I don't think it's a point of pride.

"They hate me, Arley and Mrs. Powell," Kiki says.

Before I can reply, she asks, "Can I stay here for a little while?"

"Is this because of Arley?"

"I feel bad."

"Kiki—"

"Oh, come on, Tata," Ella says. "I just checked that woman's page again. She's already talking like Kiki broke Arley's leg with her bare hands. It's not the worst idea to let her lay low here for a while."

Kiki's eyes widen and my stomach drops a bit. I'd expected a sprain, some bruising. That maybe Mrs. Powell had been exaggerating.

Kiki turns to her aunt. "It's broken?"

"Who's at the hospital with Arley?" I ask, the image of Mrs. Powell curbside still open on my phone.

"Auntie Esther," Ella says. Esther is one of the WhatsApp aunties (along with Sister Roseline). One of those older Haitian women who, with all of their kids successfully raised and in their own careers, now spend the bulk of their days correcting other people's children. Mostly through instant message, sometimes in person. They'll even offer advice after Sunday service if you're in real trouble. They're staples at every church service. I left the group chat after one of them offered to physically discipline Kiki for me ("Bring her to my house, Tata. We've beat out demons before"), but Ella's still in because she's just that nosy. If they knew about my Vodou altar, decided that that's where Kiki's demon lived, I'm sure that, in their heads, I would make the mental migration from bad mother to spiritual peril.

Ella holds her phone up to us, a picture of a brown knee so swollen that the skin looks waxy. In the photo, Arley looks dazed. Kiki's face goes gray. I look at Ella, and my impulse to ask her about her own altar is the strongest it's ever been. She watches me, and she waits. But I say nothing.

Elijah texts me again. Sister Roseline made it. The next picture he sends me is of an empty curb.

⁓

Ella and I lived with my grandfather, my mother's father, because it was easier.

My mother worked, and works, as a flight attendant. My father's visa applications have been meeting strange ends since I was two: legal help applied for the wrong one, birth certificates were missing, went to an anti-government rally where he threw a tire iron through an office window and got labeled a public threat. My grandfather had a radio announcer's voice and cooked like somebody said he couldn't. He was a Vodou priest who held all of his ceremonies in his garage, pushed boula drums against stored stepladders and old broken vacuum cleaners. Every lwa had its day, but Azaka-Tonnerre, god of thunder, had two. I loved them both. His second name, Tonnerre, is a Creole curse word, and Granpa did not allow me to say it even on Azaka-Tonerre's feast days. His main offerings are rum and smoke, but Granpa wouldn't allow either of those things into his house because of his granddaughters. He subbed them in with more fried pork (another offering of the god's), and Ella and I spent much of our adolescence sneaking into the ceremonies for Styrofoam platters of the stuff. Once, a sweaty woman who'd been possessed by Azaka grabbed my arm and asked me to shout my laughter into her face. That was our loudest day. I don't know why no one ever made a formal noise complaint against us. I think it was the fear.

It wasn't just the veneration of gods either, but our dead too. Sometimes my grandfather would speak to my grandmother, eyes rolled back so only the whites showed, while lwas couched themselves in other bodies and made them sing. The only other place I've ever seen a bodily recklessness like Kiki's was at those ceremonies, when spirits took over the guests and brought along the confidence that their flesh would not bruise and their bones would not break. I saw people throw themselves face-first into the concrete ground of my grandfather's garage and come up with their faces as intact and brown as they'd been. People climbed onto his stepladder and jumped off and landed on their knees just fine. If there was anything higher around, inside, I'm sure they would have climbed that too. In those moments, they felt like the only true things. Bodies the most solid they could be. Sometimes, my grandfather would have to abandon his conversation with my grandmother to usher out Ella and me. Too dangerous, he'd say. I've never been able to shake the suspicion that he would know something about Kiki that I do not.

My grandfather succumbed to a flu that never left. I was ten and Ella was eight. A part of me thought this form of death insulting. My Granpa's life condensed should have made a crater somewhere. Yet his cancer was so quiet that up until the very end, when Ella and I would make our Polly Pocket dolls "walk" along the edge of his hospital bed, I thought that he might get better. It was then that I learned to grieve absence with clutter. When our mother came to get us, between a red-eye to Bucharest and a midafternoon to New Orleans, I tried to bring as much as I could with me. My grandfather's hair oil, our cooking pots, the multicolored head wraps his ceremony attendees used to hand out to Ella and me like candy, the goddamn stepladder.

"No, Taya," my mother said, taking an unopened pack of candles out of my hands, "this will make it harder."

Kiki's absence from home is temporary. I know this, in my head, but my soul acts on reflex because of how well I remember that older loss. A soul reflex. A thinner mourning. As soon as I get home that day, I take a couple of the posters from Kiki's room, a few combs, a hairbrush, and put them in ours. Elijah laughs a bit when he sees me moving between rooms like this, chalks it up to a Taya thing.

"Just go get her, babe," Elijah says. "Sister Roseline handled it. We can help with some of Arley's medical expenses. It's done."

Elijah likes the finish. He hosts a solo segment at the station on Thursday and Friday afternoons. His cameraman gives him the first half of a headline, throws it onto a broad monitor, and Elijah will construct the second half from a few choice hints. He has the violent, overactive imagination of a person who grew up sheltered, so he almost always gets them right. When I was pregnant with Yani, one of the Thursday first-halves was "A massage therapist who—" and the hint was an animation of an anthropomorphic nail putting on its jeans. Elijah guessed ". . . pries off clients' nails while they're in a drugged sleep." I wonder if this is what Elijah has done now, hooked his chosen ending to our moment. I don't know how to ask this without sounding like I'm gearing up for an insult, so I say nothing.

Two days later, I'm leaving the house with Yani to go to Target. Both of her crescent moon night-lights blew out the night before and she screamed so loud that coughing took over. I've checked to make sure I have my keys on me, and I'm rebraiding an undone section of Yani's hair when a woman walks up my footpath. The sun has just collapsed past the hard line of horizon and the dusk is fresh. The woman is wearing a striped hoodie over a striped shirt, and it sort of feels like she's trying too hard to be casual. I move Yani behind me, my hand on her shoulder.

"Who's that white lady, manmi?"

The woman stands at the base of my porch steps and speaks.

"Taya Jean-Wright?"

"Yes?"

The woman reaches behind her, and I clutch Yani closer. She pulls out a sheaf of papers.

"You've been served."

We're being sued.

I ride to the Target with the papers in my glove compartment next to my proof of car insurance, with Yani telling me all about the friendship-platonic-love-triangle she'd been in the middle of at recess. I stop by Ella's house to check on Kiki. She passed her calc test. When I ask her if she's ready to come home, she pauses so long that I change the subject. Ella's Trinidadian man buys us doubles and we eat them from their foil on the back porch, curry channa staining our cheeks. I don't look at the subpoena document again until that night, in bed beside Elijah. I tell him what happened.

He exhales a long breath. "Okay. Okay, let's see."

His eyes run along the length of the paper all the way down to Count 1: Negligence. The part that reminds us in Century font that Kiki's wildness, the storm that she is, is our fault. And that who she hurts is who we hurt. Elijah and I have always shared the blame. He picked Kiki up from the swing-set situation. I was the one at the administrative school meetings. He drove her to the child's psychologist every Tuesday and Thursday. I was the one who fielded Kiki's questions—*manmi, is there something wrong with me?*—who pulled apart the therapist's ruling of *technically nothing* and kept *nothing*. I know he's thinking the same thing. I feel it in the way he holds me.

"All right," he says. He still seems to think that he knows how this will end. It's another thing we have in common, the denial thing.

His brows shoot up at the dollar amount that Mrs. Powell's team is requesting. I nod, even though he's not looking at me.

"Christ. This is . . ."

"Enough to hammer a diamond nugget into his knee." The pages cite Arley's potentially damaged athletic career. Our savings are substantial, but not substantial enough to suffer that.

Elijah breathes out harder, drags a hand down his face. He looks at me like he's asking me to make it so,

"There's no way this is gonna hold, right? They have to dismiss it."

In the morning, I go to the flea market with Kiki and Yani. Saturdays are often busy, but the sky threatens rain today. There are no lines, no elbows to dodge for the good eggplants. Sister Roseline is several stalls down from us, arguing with the vendor over green onions. I turn my back in that direction to conceal my daughters, and I hope she doesn't recognize me.

Yani picks up a yuca root from the stand in front of us, and she almost drops it because her hands are so small. The vendor wears a frown he's trying to stuff into a smile. I think that he would rip the root out of her hands if I wasn't standing right here. Yani holds the yuca up to Kiki.

"When are you coming home so I can stop pretending to like these?" she asks.

I gasp to fake offense. "Manmi's right here," I say.

Yani turns to me, face serious. "Manmi, I don't like these."

Kiki looks better, less anxious than she'd been when she'd asked to stay with her aunt. It's temporary, but the distance from Arley is helping her guilt. She, like Ella, knows to plant whatever hurts, plant it and go. Knows how to leave it hostaged by its own roots.

Kiki's eyes move to somewhere over my shoulder. When I turn around, I see Sister Roseline coming towards us. Mrs. Powell is right beside her, and I feel myself straightening up, my body braced for impact just like theirs seem to be.

"Sister Taya!" Roseline says. "How are you?"

She doesn't wait for me to answer before she's kissing my cheek, her body as far from me as it can be. Her big silver earring almost cuts into my cheek.

"We miss you over at St. Paul's! The back pews have been empty as ever."

I give her a smile that I can already sense is too much teeth. "Sorry to hear that! You sing loud enough for two churches, I'm sure I'm hardly missed."

My family's exit from St. Paul's, our local Catholic church, hadn't been premeditated. I'd been serious when I'd told Elijah, right before we got married, that I'd join. That I'd take whatever step is just below full conversion, raise our kids like that too. I was still grieving my grandfather by forgetting, then, and it was easy to agree. We didn't stop going regularly until Kiki's Vodou rattle show-and-tell case, when the kids in Sunday school started asking Kiki if she could help them find other people they'd lost, aunties in juice boxes, uncles in faucets, and Kiki would come home in tears because she could not help. The adult congregation's questions started to arise then, too: where did you get that rattle? What was it from? It looks just like something you'd use for _____, doesn't it? I told Elijah I wanted us to become those people who only go for major holidays. He agreed, and I found myself a bit offended on Jesus's behalf. *Where's your commitment?* I'd thought.

But all of that is weak in the face of this: St. Paul's is where most Haitians come to get their community news, where they cook if their stove is broken, where the neighborhood falls into itself. When we left, everyone knew, devout or not.

Sister Roseline regards me now, the hinges of her smile worn down. She reaches a hand out to Yani and Yani tucks herself behind my leg, still young enough that unfamiliar faces are frightening. Sister Roseline laughs, like it's absolutely adorable.

"Hello, Kiki," Sister Roseline says.

"Anaïca," Kiki says, erasing the familiarity. Sister Roseline laughs again, and it is forced this time. Mrs. Powell sucks her teeth. She looks at me like she wants to spit.

"This is how you raise her, ehn? To talk back?"

"She doesn't talk back to me," I say.

"Hmph. You sent her after Arley, didn't you?"

I know that I must be the adult here, but I feel my temper rising. "What?"

"Yes! You sent her after Arley because he's being scouted by top colleges, and your girl's being scouted by federal watchlists!"

Yani tightens her grip on my shirt.

"Leave my manmi out of this," Kiki says. Then, just a little bit quieter, "And I didn't do it on purpose."

"Oh?" Mrs. Powell says. "Speak that into his leg, maybe your words will heal it. You unbelievable girl."

Mrs. Powell moves to get closer to Kiki, so I do too. I push Kiki behind me as Sister Roseline holds Mrs. Powell back, tells her to *control yourself, ehn?*

After a few moments of this, Mrs. Powell stops. Chuckles a bit.

"You know what?" she says. She looks straight at me. "I will leave this to my God and my lawyer."

➥

My mother once asked me if I'd dropped Kiki when she was a baby.

This was when the elementary school first called Elijah to come pick Kiki up, when she'd taken to standing up on the seat of playground swings. My mother was visiting from Georgia, sleeping on the sofa because I'd refused to give up the locked back room where I'd arranged my grandfather's altar. When I told her where she'd be sleeping, she looked at me like I had smacked her. "I'm here and he's not, Tata," she'd said. I understood the point she was trying to make, but it sounded like a rehash of my own failure. *He is not here because you cannot bring him.* This was within the first thirty minutes of her arrival.

The second day of her trip was when she asked me the question. I looked at my mother like she was crazy. She followed it up with, "She might have gotten used to falling."

"I've never dropped her," I'd said. My voice cracked. I didn't think I had to tell my mother that Kiki was the first soft thing I'd ever made and I wrought my arms into refuge for her. She was a mother too. My mother. I thought she knew. When I carried my baby, she vignetted me, gave each sector of my body its own ache. For eight weeks my belly was nearly the same size. For months it felt like she was still corded to me. How would I have dropped her?

I'd had a talk with Kiki that night, sat her down at the dining room table with Burger King French Toast Sticks and syrup. I asked her,

"Baby, why do you like jumping so much?"

She chewed as she thought. "I just like it."

"What do you like about it?"

"I feel like a real person."

If I could have that conversation with Kiki again, *just* like that—have her be the same age, buy the same French toast from the same Burger King, everything—I would've asked her: baby, what do you mean? Elijah wanted us to fix the swing set jumping thing, to get Kiki to apologize to the teachers and other kids. To admit she hadn't done it on purpose. His insistence was what distracted me. I did not ask her what I should have. I said,

"The other kids are real people too. You could hurt them," I made myself say. "Do you understand?"

Kiki frowned a little bit, like she was trying to figure out how to tell me something. I should have helped. I carried her under my left lung for the entirety of my third trimester. She was younger then, better caked in my breath. I should have helped. But I didn't, and she said,

"Yes."

꩜

We use one of the news station's lawyers. He's the one who represented the former head anchor, Elijah's predecessor, after his DUI.

He looks like he wants to pat my head and feed me a bone-shaped biscuit every time I ask a good question. He calls Elijah *'Lijah* and tells us that he's going to file a motion to dismiss the case with a smile that, for all of its size, is hard to place. He says that it should take two to four weeks to process. I don't think the case will be thrown out, but Elijah seems to.

"No way it holds," he says as we get in the car.

"Why not?"

"Those laws are for school bullies and their parents. Kiki's not like that."

"It doesn't matter that she didn't mean it."

Elijah breathes out long, slouches back against the seat. He stares up at the car ceiling as he says,

"Why did it have to be a championship pole vaulter? Where were all the future file clerks at?"

"Elijah." I'm laughing a little bit. Elijah directs his own chuckle to the ceiling, then turns to look at me.

"Are we bad parents?"

"Don't tell me you're expecting some kinda post-performance review. We're still raising them."

His eyes smile, then his mouth does.

"What?" I ask.

"Stop trying to talk me into circles. You know I can keep up with you."

My mother always seemed like the kind of woman who would raise her children with switches and belts, but even after my grandfather died and she took us back, she wasn't around often enough for me to be sure. Sister Roseline used to tell the group chat all about how when her children were young and they misbehaved, she would discipline them with almost anything within reach: house slippers, soup ladles, clothes hangers. It was almost a brag. It was the follow-up message to the one where someone offered to correct Kiki for me. My daughter is not made up of hard, clanking things that catch the light wrong. I cannot beat her softer and I will not try.

That day, I'm nearly shoulder-checked by the history teacher at Yani's school (who insists that after-school pickup isn't in front of the gym, when I know for a fact that it is). It's not the same elementary school that Kiki went to, so there shouldn't be so much talk about the Dave & Buster's incident, but southwest Miami's not actually that big. Word gets around. One of the art teachers once asked me if I've ever cursed anyone with Vodou. Her eyes asked me her real question—*have you ever killed anything?* Yet I can't help but think that this school is better than the alternative. For a while when Yani was four, right before she started school, Elijah's mother was very set on placing her in a private Catholic one. She'd long since taken to blaming Kiki's strangeness on the poverty of the public school system. "They give the kids expired milk!" had been a common refrain.

"Would it bother you?" Elijah asked me then. When we were little, Ella would use her bike to chase down the kids who left decapitated rubber chickens on our porch step every Halloween. Maybe if I was strong like that my answer would've been no.

"Yes," I said.

I stop by Ella's house that day with Yani and Elijah. Kiki comes out to greet us and Yani bolts from the backseat like she's been shot from a cannon. They rope their father into a game of tag on the lawn. After dinner, her father asks her whether she's ready to come home. It's his turn to be met with a silence that makes him change the subject.

That night in my house, restless, I get up from bed and I go to the back-room altar with a soft hand towel to do some dusting. The objects at the altar, even if I cannot call my grandfather down with them, are comforting. I wipe the dust from the unlit candle's exterior as its cool glass steals my heat.

I would not call the back-room altar a compromise between Elijah and me. It's a room that makes Elijah uncomfortable, and his discomfort offends me, and he's only agreed to its presence because he loves me. When I told him seven months ago that I'd stop going inside the room, after I'd caught cramps in my thighs from trying to summon my grandfather for five hours straight, he looked relieved. It was slight, but I caught it.

I come to my knees and close my eyes and move the rattle so gently I can barely hear it. I grip my thigh and I hope to convulse. I wait for Kiki's answers. But I come out of the room with nothing new. Elijah is in the hallway, caught in a spill of light from the bathroom.

"Taya? I thought you said . . ."

"I'm not allowed to clean it?"

The judge denies the motion to dismiss. It only takes them a week to decide.

Elijah's on shift, so the lawyer calls me. Just as I get off the phone with him, I look out of the living room window and notice the short line of women ribboning into Mrs. Powell's house. I recognize Auntie Roseline even from here, the straight back, the royal blue head wrap that's essentially a part of her. The other WhatsApp aunties. I barely resist the urge to duck under the sill.

When I tell Elijah about the decision on the motion, he looks so surprised that I think he will lose his eyebrows to his hairline. We meet with the TV-anchor-DUI lawyer the following day. He tells us that the motion was dismissed on the basis that Elijah and I were both aware of the threat that Kiki presented, but didn't take reasonable steps to control her behavior.

"She's not malicious!" Elijah insists.

"Hey, I'm right there with you 'Lijah."

A vein in my forehead twitches.

"What's next?" I ask.

"A deposition. We'll have to figure out exactly what happened that day. Mrs. Powell's side will question your daughter and your side will question Arley."

"Is there any precedent for her behavior?" the lawyer asks.

Elijah and I are too quiet for too long. I can tell we both want to look at each other. The lawyer doesn't flinch. Telling him about the swing-set thing is simpler. Elijah handles that. The rattle incident doesn't seem to count; Elijah doesn't bring it up and neither will I. But I don't know how to explain the other thing. The way she broke her ankle. How to explain that whenever I drive past the commercial horse-riding trail on my way to work, I think of my heart hiked up my throat. Of back then. Of the first time I'd ever seen her jump. Of Kiki standing up in the stirrups as her horse sped up to a gallop before her guide could say or do anything. How I ran forward when her foot got stuck, right before she, somehow, freed herself from the stirrups and braced her hands against the horse's neck in a single fluid motion. How she looked when she jumped and stuck weightless in open space for half a second, beautiful and brown and in danger and mine.

We spend that afternoon in Ella's backyard, Ella and I on the porch while the girls play in the grass. Elijah has been called in to work the Breaking News Center.

The girls are tossing around a tennis ball, one of the novelty ones that Ella got from a tournament in Gitega. Yani, despite her size, throws it long. It whips towards the fence, past Kiki, and Kiki runs after it. Chases it, till she slams shoulder first into the wood of the barrier. I flinch.

"Anaïca!" I say. By the time I get to Kiki and Yani in the grass, Kiki's turning the ball over in her hand, explaining to her sister that tennis balls are yellow because yellow's easier to see through TV screens. She tells me that her shoulder's fine. I hover.

I pull her aside and tell her the news. This is nothing like when she jumps or falls; I can check her arms or legs and track the true weight of her pain. I can try to ignore my pride at the fact that she surfaces intact. When I tell her about the deposition, I can track none of that weight.

"I'm gonna see Arley?" she asks. Her face is graying.

"Just for a little while," I say. She watches me like she's waiting. The clear, big-eyed look that says that manmi (or daddy) will fix this because they've always done so before. My arms are my non-answer. I wrap them around her and pull her into me.

❧

Yani and I fall asleep at Ella's house that night because there is no school the next day. I manage some sort of text to Elijah. Something with smileys and exclamation points, so there's no doubt that we're okay.

I'm sleeping in Ella's guest room, my nose full of Downy, when I feel someone's hand on my shoulder. I open my eyes to a nighttime dark molded to the window and Ella standing over me.

"I need to show you something," she says.

"Now?"

"Yes, now. We're still trying to do this whole bonding thing, right?"

She brings me into her bedroom. The bed has been pushed up against the wall to clear as much space as possible. She's moved all of the stuff from the top of her drawer, thrown it onto her bed instead. Made a makeshift altar so similar to the one I have in my own back room. Except the rattle looks smoother than hard plastic and the candles are long, white, and nondescript. There is a framed photo of my grandfather leaning against the vanity mirror. He's wearing a Panama hat with his foot raised and braced on a chair, grinning. My mother never let us keep any of them, so similar in grieving approach to Elijah and his family. I wonder how Ella got her hands on this one. My throat feels thick.

"It's never worked when I've tried it."

"Maybe you forgot some stuff. I have too. Maybe we can fill in the blanks for each other." Ella takes my hand and leads me to the dresser. She hands me a rattle and lights the incense.

We kneel in close to each other, gathered together like fingers in a fist. I turn to my Granpa's picture, and I pray truths too ugly for

Elijah's god. The first? That when Kiki crashed into Arley outside of that D&B, ruptured him, a part of me wishes that I could have watched.

We Feel It in Punta Cana

It happens like this. These are the days when the tile in the patio gets so hot it feels like I'm walking across the sun. When I'm going outside to get the stuff that Juanma brought from the store, and the air's so thick it's like I'm running downward through a rain that's never done falling. I wouldn't run but we live up a hill, and the driveway's really long, so Juanma never wants to bring the car all the way up to the house. I wouldn't run but Don Rodrigo hates it when the milk from the store comes back too warm.

I'm walking through the patio and Don Rodrigo is sitting at the glass table, reading his newspaper, all the way on the other side of the sun. The beach and the trees are behind him and I'm thinking that it looks all wrong. I'm thinking that if he's gonna take his café at his glass table on top of a star then the only thing that should be up against his back is the dark. Rafi told me once while he was doing his homework that you can't hear anything in space. That you could shout your throat out but nothing would happen.

That's what I'm thinking about when the plate falls out of my hands. I don't feel it when it slips. It's like falling asleep—one minute you're awake and the next all that loud inside your head is snapping open to let the quiet through. One minute I'm holding it. The next I'm not. I don't hear the plate break, I feel it. This house is me, this tile's the floor of my chest.

Don Rodrigo looks up from his newspaper and looks at me. I'm remembering that one time when I was little that I took the hill too fast, and I started to fall. The grass sliding across my legs, the dirt all over me, the blood I could taste in my mouth when my head hit the gravel at the bottom. All I wanted to do then was be on the other side of what was happening. I wanted to be on the side that would let me forget.

But I'm feeling it all right now, with Don Rodrigo looking through me. I wonder what he's seeing today. Sometimes I'm his little negrito, his niño listo. The best of my people, the first Haitian helper they've had here who never, ever cries even though he (who is me) is so young. Never cries, even when the nighttime comes and they're sleeping in the back room closest to the chicken shed. Sometimes Don Rodrigo calls me into the living room from the kitchen and reads the newspaper to me.

Do you know who the president is?

No, Don Rodrigo. (I always say, even though I do. Don Rodrigo is happy happy happy when he's telling me things he thinks I don't know.)

Well, it's un hombre de calidad, Leonel Hernandez.

And he'll look at me and I'll give him the surprise he needs to see. I'll draw it on my face, like Rafi and me used to draw those houses in the dirt outside, with fallen sticks from the bannann tree, when we were really little.

He's done a lot for your people.

Sí, Don Rodrigo.

I've done a lot for your people.

Muchas gracias, Don Rodrigo. Que dios le bendiga.

But I'm thinking, right now, while I'm looking at Don Rodrigo's eyes light like the moon, that this is not going to be one of those times. I don't say sorry because I know it will make it worse, whatever's coming. When it rains too hard here all the cars go too fast. Juanma tells me it's harder to drive. Whatever I say right now, it'll be the rain.

What scares me the most, while I'm watching Don Rodrigo get up from the table in the patio, is how quiet his face is. It's like the pool outside in the backyard when no one's using it.

Doña Carla hit me once, when I was smaller, when I forgot to sweep under the stairs. It was a slap. I think she wanted me to fall down but I didn't. I had a bruise, and Don Rodrigo told her to never do it again. Juanma hit me once, just on the arm, when I crossed the street on our way to the mercado without looking and a guagua almost hit me. Manuela slapped me with a kitchen towel one time when I didn't turn off the stove quick enough and the red beans almost burned.

But Don Rodrigo has never hit me, not ever. He's walking up to me now, a big mustache dark gray like the ash from his cigarettes. He has never hit me, not ever. I'm wondering if he's going to try to make up for it. I'm wondering if there's a closet inside him somewhere, where he's been keeping all those times he wanted to hit me like Doña Carla did.

He grabs my arm, hard, right below my shoulder. I can't help it, I flinch.

No te muevas. He says it through his teeth.

He has his hand so tight around me. He pulls me through the living room, past all the paintings with the white people and their ash-from-cigarettes mustaches. Past the couches, past the little table in the middle of the room.

Then we're outside, out on the street, and Don Rodrigo is pulling me towards his big white car. I've barely ever seen him drive it because Juanma always does. Rafi told me what the people in the US call it but I can't remember. When Don Rodrigo grabs my arm tight it's like he's grabbing the throat of every day I've lived before this one. My past. I can't remember anything with him. There's always only the now, only the coming.

Don Rodrigo throws me into the back of the car, and gets into the front seat. The driver's seat. Where's Juanma?

He takes off down the street and I want to close my eyes but I can't. We're driving through Punta Cana, down past all the white houses, the ones smaller than where Don Rodrigo lives. The pink and yellow and purple houses, the ones bigger than where Don Rodrigo lives. The ones where the white people stay when they come to visit. One of them gave me a dollar once when I was walking to the mercado. I still have it, folded up under my bed somewhere.

We're driving past the beaches, past the white people with no clothes on. Past the pretty girls with the curly hair and skin like café con mucha leche. Past the big store where Juanma does all the food shopping. Past Rafi's school. Past Doña Carla's salon.

Past everything until we're in a place I've never seen before. There are trees everywhere, as far as I can see. They make the streets back home seem naked. Sometimes I would see places like this on Rafi's TV, and when I asked him where they were, he would look at me all surprised and say, right here, in Santo Domingo. Right here. Not there, from the other side where I'm from.

Don Rodrigo is driving down a skinny gravel road between the trees and it's so bright out that I'm thinking this is where it happens. This is the part of Santo Domingo the sun goes to when it leaves home. Yes, we feel it in Punta Cana. I'm sure other people in other places feel it too. But it's always, always on its way here.

We're driving for a long time. The green leaves of all the trees make a ceiling, and some sunlight pokes through until it feels like we're riding through one of those boxes with all the holes. The ones you put lizards in when you want to keep them but you don't want them to die.

We drive so long that I think if I wasn't so scared I'd be asleep. Then the trees end, and we're driving up to a bunch of houses. But I've never seen houses like this before. They're tiny and faded, with roofs that look like they might be made of tin foil, like the vegetable stalls in the mercado. All the little roads that I can see, the ones that run between the houses, are like the desert roads in Rafi's movies. The ones where the cowboys do all their shooting.

A little shirtless Black boy runs past Don Rodrigo's car. Don Rodrigo pulls up in front of a green house with a rusty roof. He gets out the car and walks around to my side. My heart's beating hard but steady inside me, like if it doesn't go too fast he might forget all about me. Can he hear my heart inside me? Does it sound like Rafi's football hitting the chain fence in the backyard? Is it one of Manuela's pots falling off the counter and hitting the ground of the kitchen? Does it make him want to grind his teeth, does it make the hair on the back of his neck stand up, does it make his head hurt?

He's pulling me out of the car now. He makes me stand in front of the house while he walks across the street, to the little boy from before. A small Black girl with a dirty red shirt on walks up to me. Her eyes are so bright I could see them in the dark. They're like lanterns.

And she tells me that nunca te he visto aquí, and I tell her that it's because no soy de aquí. She looks confused, and she reaches out her tiny hand to me. She puts it on my wrist and lets me know that todos los negros viven aquí, todos en el mundo.

She throws some half-memories out into the street of me. I know that they're made up, I've lived with Don Rodrigo forever. But I make up this beautiful nighttime woman in my head, this woman that looks like me, and she's wearing a dress like those trees we drove through. She's wearing the leaves and all that sunlight's cutting through them, cutting through her. And through the million little windows the sun makes in her I can see Don Rodrigo coming back to my side of the street, his hand tight around that little boy's throat. The boy's scratching at Don Rodrigo's wrists, and Don Rodrigo drags him all the way back to me.

Then they're standing in front of me, Don Rodrigo and the boy. Don Rodrigo is squeezing and squeezing with a face like a cloudless sky. The boy's still scratching at his wrist and my ribs are tossing my heart around, throwing it back and forth inside me.

I'm screaming. I've never spoken much louder than a whisper around Don Rodrigo, not once. But now I'm screaming like those ladies on TV who watch their sons get shot down in front of them. I'm screaming like those white girls in the movies when they're watching the knife come for them. I'm screaming and it's a sound like metal against metal, like a steel nail coming down hard against a glass window. The little girl is crying. I'm begging him to,

Para! Para! Por dios, para!

Everybody's outside now, men and women and boys and girls standing in front of their houses, scared, watching Don Rodrigo. The boy's eyes are closed when Don Rodrigo lets go. The boy falls to the ground. He's not moving, but through my tears, when I get a little closer, I can see that he's breathing.

Don Rodrigo turns to me, his face still like the pool behind the house when no one's using it. He's looking right at me, and I can't stop crying. He rolls the sleeves of his white shirt back down. Rafi read one of his fantasy books to me a while ago, and it said that god fell out of the sky and into the ocean once. He never stopped being embarrassed and now he hates the water and anyone who goes into it for too long and that's why so many people die in the water. I'm looking up and I'm thinking that maybe Don Rodrigo pushed him.

He drops a heavy hand on my shoulder, and I can barely see him through my cloudy eyes but I keep looking.

Ten cuidado mi negrito, he says, and I can't see his face but his voice bounces around from my ribs to my arms to my legs. He tells me, this is where you would be without me. This is what a person could come here and do to you without me. Pues, ten cuidado mi negrito y walk slower.

Eli

You never really know what your mind's gonna run to when you're dropped in the middle of a perfect quiet. I'm walking down Sherman and Main, about to hit the bookstore, and the sky's staring back at me blue as anything, like somebody took a slice of the hottest star they could find and wrapped it around the world. It's a weird sky. No clouds, no sun, just this unbelievable ice blue like the world's folding in on itself, all those glaciers at the poles tearing through the air right above my head.

But even with the cold sky hanging over everything, everybody around me is wrapped up in their happiness. It's zipped up to their necks. A girl with a shaved blonde head rolls a stroller past, and she's laughing on the phone with someone. Across the street a sweet-looking old lady is sitting on a park bench reading a newspaper, and I start to smile until I realize the newspaper's about the urban problem. But I know the day's quiet when my biggest issue's an elderly Asian lady reading a racist paper. A blue Civic drives by just as I'm reaching the flower shop at the intersection, and it's blasting "All Along the Watchtower," the Jimi Hendrix version.

I'm wondering, not for the first time, if the Fro-Yo Palace is open right now. Yeah, it's only like 9:00 a.m. but cravings are cravings, and I woke up on the side of the bed that had me itching for a cup of Mega Berry Blast like a motherfucker.

I'm coming up on this lady in a super nice fall coat when somebody, can't tell you who it is, pulls the bag over my head. Shock is different for everyone, like fingerprints. You can speculate about it all you want, but you can't ever know what you'd do if some scary shit happened to you until it actually happens. Me, my shock brings that quiet with it. Silence wraps itself around my skull like a wet towel till the only sounds I can recognize are inside the cramped room of my head.

I can't hear anything that's going on around me, can't make sense of any of the noises that aren't already inside me. I imagine people shouting, screaming like you do before you realize just how bad things actually are, when fear's just blurry and indistinct. Before anybody turns the resolution up to like one hundred and you realize exactly *why* and *how* you're fucked.

My mind runs home, runs to that time Bryce was chasing me through the house and face-planted into the tile, gave himself a bloody nose that he couldn't really blame anybody else for. Then it's chasing after that one time Ana and I went around the kitchen, pulled out as many things we could find, flour, sugar, cinnamon, allspice, and baked all of it into one big stomach bomb. I still have no idea how we didn't have the runs for the rest of our natural-born lives. Then it's trying to reach one of those million times I went into my mami's room while she was lying down watching TV, climbed into her bed and used her stomach as a pillow while HGTV played like muted rain behind me. The forever soundtrack to my saturday nights.

The amount of time it takes for them to snatch me and throw me into the back of that car? I'd have to say it rounds out to about forty-five seconds. But I cross *days* inside my head. Isn't that wild?

I feel the big hands tight around my biceps, feel my shoulder hit an armrest when whoever it is that grabs me tosses me into the backseat like a bookbag (always was the weaker son; what a fucking joke). So I'm facedown in the backseat for a little bit, my shoulder one wrong rollover away from snapping like a twig. The car speeds up and I feel someone behind me, tying my arms behind my back so my forearms are pressed up against each other. They sit me up. No one's talking and all I can think is wow, are kidnappers supposed to be this quiet? The person next to me, the one that sat me up, speaks, and it's a guy. He sounds more like somebody three-quarters of the way through their eight-hour at the DMV than anything else when he says,

"Don't scream."

I could laugh. Like I could scream even if I wanted to. Like my voice isn't hiding from me, deep inside my chest where fear's growing like a forest between my ribs.

And the sack. The damn sack over my head. Jesus, I'd really taken it for granted, hadn't I? Breathing open air. My whole head is hot, and I feel like I'm gonna pass out. And I do. I fall into Big Guy's lap, and what little dignity I had left runs out into the street to get hit by a semitruck.

❧

I wake up to a loud purple room. The brightness is a little undercut by the peeling lavender paint, and for a second I think the walls are melting. I shift a little, and I realize my arms are still tied tight, except this time they're wrapped behind the back of the chair I'm sitting in. I'm looking out at the room now through eyes like foggy glass, at the rickety-ass wooden table in front of me with all the scratches on its surface, at the blacked-out window just a few feet past it, and I'm thinking, kind of bizarrely, that this is what that interrogation room in the Bahamas must have looked like to my dad. He used to tell me a bunch of stuff, used to say that in the Caribbean, color pools in all of life's parts, collects everywhere like runoff. No matter what happens there, good or bad, it happens hard, with more force than you could ever imagine.

But I'm not in Nassau right now (I don't think?) and I'm not my dad (I thank God). There's a sad little bulb hanging from the ceiling, trying its level best to do the work of a better light. Except for the chair I'm sitting in and the tiny table, the room's empty.

I'm wrong though, because when I blink again, when all those things in my line of vision, the purple paint, the table, the slate-gray cement floor, press up against each other and reality snaps closed behind them like a heavy vault door, I see the kid sitting in the corner. He's in one of those white plastic chairs, the kind that can't make it through a single barbecue without the legs bowing and splitting.

His head's turned away from me, and he's staring at one of the blackout windows like he's waiting for the sun to come.

If you're looking at his face he's around the same age as me. Pretty like a girl, the kind of face the douchebags I hung out with in junior high would've had a field day with. But his eyes age him. They're blacker than those bits of the universe light can't touch. Creepy in that sad kind of way, like a house people can't live in anymore.

And get this—the first thing I feel, looking at the kid who's been tasked with *literally keeping me hostage*, is a little pity. Just a little, enough to throw me for a loop. The guy looks too much like those half-naked little kids we'd see sometimes when mami drove too far downtown, the ones wearing sneakers that looked like they were one tag game away from falling apart.

One time we were driving downtown past the farmer's market, mami, Bryce, and I (Ana was still a baby then; mami had left her home with the nanny). I must've been six or seven, which would've made Bryce nine or ten. While we were waiting at the intersection, waiting for the light to turn green, a Buick came in from the street to our left, blew right through the intersection, hit a little brown girl as she was crossing the street with her mom and an older lady I took to be her grandma. The Buick stopped. Some tall guy got out of it, some investment-banker, I'd-foreclose-on-your-house-at-the-drop-of-a-hat type. He was dressed in a black suit. And yeah, I was little, but I'll never forget this—the guy walked up to the family, to the sobbing mom and grandma, took out his wallet, and offered them some bills. The mom was crouched over her unconscious little girl on the street, too distraught to pay attention to the guy. But the grandma? Oh, you should've seen that little old lady. Imagine this—an elderly woman in a pressed black wig and a pink floral print church dress launching herself at some guy twice her size. I don't know how many times she hit him in the face (my memory says four or five) before he pushed her back and she fell.

Mr. Buick threw the bills down at the ground, at the family, got back into his car, and drove away. When our light turned green and mami drove past, I looked out at the window and watched as the mom picked up her unconscious little girl and walked back over to the sidewalk, the grandma limping behind her. The wind picked up the scattered money, and I watched green paper swirl around itself.

Mami never talked about it. Bryce tried to bring it up once, a few weeks after it happened, but she gave him this look that made him never want to bring it up again. And me? I was still little so I couldn't understand exactly what had happened, but I knew how it made me feel. It made me nauseous to think about it, so I made sure I never did. Till now, staring up at this kid who has *downtown* written all over his field coat with all those damn pockets. All over his jeans, his boots, his face. And now I'm looking for anything, anything at all, that might tamp down the nausea. I need some-thing to swallow up all that empty space in my head, because that morning at the intersection is trying to live inside it.

"Hey," I call out.

He looks over at me and I'm thinking, damn, maybe he *would've* been able to handle those assholes I went to school with.

He doesn't say anything, just looks at me like he's waiting for me to finish. I'm surprised by how self-conscious that makes me feel. Now I gotta choose whatever I'm gonna say carefully, make sure it lands somewhere inside that tenuous middle ground of *you're so fucking screwed* and *but actually, can you tell me where the hell I am?*

I was scared before, when they pulled that sack over my head and threw me into the back of that car. But now that my heart's not beating so fast inside me, now that there's not some huge guy with his hands tight around my arms, I'm mostly just annoyed. Irritated. Tired. Mentally emotionally spiritually exhausted. My dad—*God*, that fucking asshole.

"So," I start, but my voice comes out rough. I clear my throat and try again. "I'm *assuming* you're not just gonna tell me where I am, without any prompting?"

He's completely still for a moment, and I'm immediately on my guard. Then, he gets up, long black hair sliding across his face like the ocean on the sand when the tide comes in. He's coming towards me and I'm shuffling through all the cabinets in my head, looking for that hatred I should probably have for my dad. Trying to figure out where I left it. He walks around me, and the flat cold of a tiny blade brushes my wrist. The tension lets up in my arms when the binding snaps, and I bring my hands into my lap to rub the feeling back into them. The kid walks back around me, takes his seat. He's looking at the window again.

"Can I take that as a sign of good faith, then?"

He glances at me out of the corner of his eye. Well, now that we're doing around sixty down this road to friendship, I decide it's as good a time as ever to keep going.

"You trust me not to run?"

He doesn't even look at me when he says, "No trust. I'd catch you."

Doesn't matter that it's probably true. "You don't know that." It's quiet again. Then, "Okay, so you didn't untie me because you trust me. Why then?"

"Because you're not a prisoner."

I look around the room that I can't leave, the peeling purple paint like a sunset cage.

"Well, you're doing a real good job of convincing me otherwise."

He's looking at me directly now, and those stupid eyes are the most unreadable things I've ever seen. That static dark the earth sits in.

"You're not a prisoner, you're a hostage."

"That really clears things up."

He looks at me, unimpressed. "You hold onto a prisoner because it hurts them. You hold on to a hostage because you need them."

"And why do you need me?" I ask, like I didn't have the answer as soon as those people threw me into the back of that car. And the kid's looking back at me while the truth's just glaring at the both of us, petulant. The truth's a brat. Who knew?

Instead of answering me, the kid gets up and grabs the plastic chair. He moves into the corner right next to me, right across from the door. He's frowning a little now, but I can't really imagine what's brought on the sudden mood change. I like to think I've been just as annoying from the beginning of this conversation as I have at its end.

He breathes, "Your commentary," under his breath, and the door bangs open.

A guy in a green plaid shirt is standing in the doorway, and he looks like he should be walking his kindergartners to school, not aiming a two-tone 9mm at my fucking head. And you know what the crazy thing is? I can tell you what color his eyes are, brown like cold coffee, like packed earth after the hard rain lets up and not a moment before. I can tell you he didn't shave that morning. I can tell you his hair's wet with sweat, but not because he's nervous about what he's trying to do. No, he's ready for that. The room's hot, the room is so hot it's like the thick air is sitting in my lap, pressing up against my chest like a person.

The barrel of a gun. Looking into that kid's eyes is like staring down the barrel of a gun, when you know the bullet's there, you *know* it, but you can't see it for shit.

I don't even get a full breath out before that kid's tackling me to the floor, and the bullet meant for my head hits the wall behind me.

Looks like my right shoulder's getting no love today. It slams into the floor before my face can. My heart's beating heavy inside my chest and one two three milliseconds later, my shoulder's hurting so bad that I'm kind of wishing that guy hadn't missed.

Pain's trying to bring a hazy film over my eyes, but I still see it when the kid jumps up, fast as anything. Through the blur he's pulling out his own gun, pulling the trigger before Green Plaid even has a chance to realize he missed me. I might not be able to see all that well, but that shot is the loudest thing in the world.

Damn. He really would have caught me.

The body hits the floor, and the kid walks up to it, looks down. It twitches, so he aims for the head and shoots again.

No hesitation. The kid didn't wait a single *second* before—Oh my god. I'm laying on the concrete floor with my (probably broken, *at least* sprained) shoulder under me and I'm thinking *oh my god*. Green Plaid doesn't move again. I'm staring at the soles of his loafers, and they remind me *so fucking much* of those stupid little racetracks Bryce and I used to play with when we were really little. I'm gonna cry. I'm gonna throw up. I'm gonna shatter.

He walks over to where I'm laying on my side. Kneels down, wraps my good arm around his neck and helps me to my feet, as careful as anything. When he rips a strip of fabric off his shirt to tie it around my eyes, something's rattling inside of me. I'm looking forward to the chance to not see anything at all for a little while, even though everything in front of me is cast in that blurriness that rides in with the pain. The murkiness I'm still telling myself isn't tears waiting for me to let them through.

He leads me out of the room. The air outside's probably warm at best, but after all that heat it's gorgeously cold against my neck. I never knew the sound of crickets singing could make me feel so relieved.

We walk for days months years. Time stacks up on itself inside my head, entire bricks of it piled up so high I'm afraid it's gonna cut through the sky, leave the earth open and raw. We were walking on concrete and asphalt before, now we're on soft dirt. Something like a leaf brushes up against my face. We stop, and I hear the kid take something out of his pocket. A little while later I hear him say,

"They found us."

Some chattering on the other line fills in the nighttime quiet. Then the kid says,

"Okay."

He leans me up against a tree, on my good side. I can hear him crunching some dead leaves underfoot while he walks away from me. He's not gonna leave me in the middle of the woods with a broken shoulder, is he? This isn't any way to treat your hostages. I hear nothing, and then I hear a smashing, like a . . . is that a rock? I hear something like a rock hitting a . . . I guess that makes sense. When he's done smashing the phone, I can hear him walking up to me again. There's a reservoir pooling up inside my head. Oh *fuck* it's gonna happen. I can feel my eyes getting hot, and it scares the shit out of me. So I do that thing I always do when I'm scared shitless—I talk till I can't feel the fear anymore.

"Can you walk?"

His voice is too loud for the dark.

"As romantic as it was to have my arm draped around your neck, the answer's yes."

"I already knew you could talk," he mutters. He grabs my good elbow and leads me from the tree.

"How's your shoulder?"

"How would your shoulder be if you got tackled into hard cement?"

I'm half expecting him to lead me into a tree, just to spite me.

He breathes out hard and it sounds kind of like a chuckle. "Actually, I don't think it ever healed quite right."

I don't know what to do with this, this thing that's hanging between us that's equal parts him and me. You're not supposed to have anything in common with the people that hurt you. My dad's face keeps coming up in front of my blindfold and I can't blink him away.

We walk for a thousand years. When we stop again, the kid leans me up against another tree, and I hear a door creak open. Then he's grabbing me, telling me to *get down on my knees* and bringing my good hand to the cold rung of a ladder. My shoulder pain's still knocking hard at the door of me, so it takes me a little while to realize that we're at an underground bunker.

"Sooo," I say, fingers drumming on the metal rung, "you got a plan for getting me down there?"

"I do," he starts off, slow, "but you're not gonna like it."

He's right. I hate it. Moments later I'm on this kid's back, uninjured arm wrapped around his neck for dear life while my other arm's hanging against my side. I swear I can feel the whole thing throbbing, and the blood in my head falls into its rhythm. And then I can't help it, I'm thinking of Ana, when she was really little. When she used to jump onto my back, and I used to run up and down the house with her tiny fists tight in the fabric of my shirt, her laughs hitting the tile underneath our feet, coming back up so loud the whole house sounded like her.

Our dad used to come see us every few weeks, back before mom took us and left. He used to stagger his visits, make sure he and his shipments were never in the state at the same time. When I was little, I used to think he was a private investigator, like Magnum. When Ana was little, I let her think it too. Sometimes the truth doesn't come up to meet you. Sometimes it waits for you on the top shelf till you get big enough, tall enough, old enough to reach it. Bryce loves dad with that kind of sighted love that turns whatever it actually sees into the shit it wants to see. The man could blow up the space station on a whim and Bryce would tell you all about how NASA had it coming.

It's kind of impressive how quickly the kid makes it to the

ground with me on his back, but soon I'm down in the bunker, and he's climbing back up the ladder to close the door. I'm standing in the dark until he steps out into the bunker again and takes off my blindfold.

"Guess I wasn't missing out on much," I say when I'm blinking against the blackness of the bunker.

He finds the light switch, and there's a plastic card table with two rough metal chairs at the center of the room. There's a little stove in the corner, right next to an old wooden dresser. I don't notice that there's a little fridge, too, until the kid's walking towards it. I stumble over to one of the chairs before I can collapse. My eyesight's better now, but with that little development comes all the shit that just happened in that purple room. It's all sprinting down the hallways of my head now, coming up at me. I'm staring at the kid's back while he's kneeling down, scraping some ice from the sad little freezer inside the fridge. Where'd he put the gun? Bang, then the full wet sound of softness coming down into hardness. Could've been me, blood like paint on that cement. Would he cry for me? Could tears live inside a person like that?

The kid takes off his thin bomber jacket, and I can see the place on his shirt where my makeshift blindfold came from. He scoops some ice into his jacket, then turns back to me. His black black eyes are eating up the light, he's his own singularity. I wish I could be infinitely dense like that, wish I could fall through the earth, sink through its core, cut this planet so deep it could never heal.

He hands me the ice pack he made, and I take it, hold it up against my shoulder. I must be more delirious with pain and shock than I thought, because before long I'm saying,

"I know you."

He raises a brow. "Really?"

"I know kids like you. Guys like my dad . . . they love kids like you."

"Guys like your dad . . ." he repeats.

"Yeah. You work for one, right? Wolf."

It feels weird to say it. I knew it, had known it from the moment that big guy told me not to scream. Wolf is the only person who could ever be this bold, the only person batshit crazy enough to snatch one of Solomon's kids, on their way to get some damn fro-yo. Someone should've told him that he'd gotten the wrong kid, though. That if he really wanted to get a rise out of my dad, *don't snatch Kit, snatch Bryce.* Sure, with me, he'd be a little annoyed about having to pay the ransom, but with Bryce . . . with Bryce he would've razed the entire surface of this planet, Wolf and his assholes right along with it. He would've dared God to come down and see, if He dared.

He breathes out hard again, that chuckle. "Kids like me scare the shit out of you. It's okay though. They scare the shit out of me too." He slouches back into his chair, stares up at the ceiling. "I would've starved without guys like your dad."

His voice is rigid, like it's doing the twin work of trying to convince both himself and me.

I shift, bring the ice pack a little harder into my shoulder.

"Kind of sounds like you wish you had."

He brings his head down to look at me, and I don't really know when his eyes stopped creeping me out. Now the sadness I see there makes my heart want to catch fire inside my chest, burn its way out my body until I can't ever feel for somebody again like I feel for this long-haired kid with the girl's face sitting right across from me.

"You know what it's like to be hungry for two weeks straight? Give me the nine mil to the head."

That's what does it. Breaks all the levees inside my head, makes the tears inside me swell up and surge until I feel like I could drown inside myself. I'm holding the ice pack to my shoulder and I feel the tears coming down my cheeks. I can't even wipe them away because *I'm holding the ice pack to my fucking shoulder.* I feel the pain from my shoulder and the nausea from that day and the fear from that purple room and the sadness for this kid whirling up inside me, dissolving into my blood and my bones until my body's made up of every shitty thing I've ever felt.

Over the sound of my heart cracking inside me I hear the kid say something. He says, softly,

"You've never been hungry." And I know it's not a question but I answer anyway. I shake my head. He doesn't even sound bitter. This kid should be bitter. So, so angry. Why does it feel like I'm madder than he is?

Through my tears, I choke out, "It's fucked up."

He laughs. "You're crying for me, Kit?"

I squeeze my eyes shut tight, press the ice pack into my shoulder until it hurts. I cry harder.

Open House

Ezra sees a man with his face in the pasta section of the store that Friday. It's after school. The guy's standing there, trying to choose between some Crisco and some Mazola, and Ezra feels like the world's stopping around him, freckling into stillness. Just like it should when you see yourself, like really *see* yourself for the first time. He's happy that Angel's in the bathroom right now, wouldn't want the kid to see him like this. 'Cause he *knows* that for all the world, he looks like an idiot, hanging out next to the flour with his arms down his sides and his eyes big like twin moons.

What they don't tell you about seeing yourself like this, looking at somebody and knowing that they have your mouth or your nose or your eyebrows, is that it's nothing like looking into a mirror. Your reflection can't help but do whatever you do, it's stuck with you, trapped by you. It's tied to you like that. It needs you—that's one of those forever truths that just *is*, like Chips Ahoy cookies tasting like the plastic they come in or walking outside one day and just knowing that something bad is gonna happen, tasting that shit in the air. Nothing could've prepared Ezra for this. For seeing his cheeks and his eyelashes and his forehead dancing just outside the easysafe orbit of his control.

For watching his mouth breathe out while he's breathing in.

". . . shopping carts. Zee? Zee?"

Angel's back, and he's in Ezra's face. Ezra jumps, and his cheeks get hot.

"Did you hear me, dude? All the shelves in the bread aisle are empty. Let's go climb that shit before Nico comes back."

The man's walking away now, holding his Crisco.

Ezra turns to Angel. "That guy looks just like my dad."

Angel looks confused. Ezra can tell. It's such a weird look on him, his eyebrows falling together like that. Angel gets excited, angry, irritated, irritat*ing*. Never confused, never lost. You'd think the kid has the world's original blueprints on him, mint condition, he's so damn sure of everything. But now he's looking at Ezra like he can't really figure him out.

He says, "I thought you didn't know what your dad looks like."

"I mean, yeah," Ezra agrees. The words come up his throat feverish. "But that guy kind of looks like what I think my dad might look like. That guy looks like me."

"Oh." Angel frowns. "Do you think—?"

"No."

Later, when they're in one of the checkout lines, waiting to buy some Hot Pockets while Nico's staring at them like they're the reason he's still single, Ezra sees the man again. Angel does too, but he doesn't say anything about it.

". . . Italian army." The man is talking to this lady in line, has been for a little while now, and Ezra doesn't hear any other piece of their conversation. But he hears that.

Ezra and Angel are walking the three blocks back home, just passing the check cashing place, when something starts to burn up hot and sharp inside Ezra's stomach. He thinks about that question *can you miss something that you've never had* and he knows the answer is yes like he knows the weekend is coming. Like he knows what his own pulse feels like.

Fourteen years of nothing, then, *boom*, his heart wants to burst and take the rest of his body along with it. What a gag.

He's the one who comes up with the idea, with a singular, cosmic ambition that could make a Big Tobacco exec sweat.

But Angel doesn't sweat most things, and the kid just eats it right up when Ezra suggests it. They're sitting out on Angel's patio in plastic chairs, and Ezra doesn't know what's louder, the traffic down on the street or Angel's brothers and sisters inside the apartment.

"*Sabotage?*" Angel's eyes are lighting up.

Ezra laughs. "Yeah."

"Aw, man," Angel shifts in his seat. "Why didn't I think of this before? Zay sucks at choosing people to live here. I mean, when Brook left . . ." He trails off, and his eyes get a little dark, like the inside of your car does when you're driving at night and you move past the street lamps.

Ezra looks out over the edge of the balcony, watches a gray Civic blow right through the intersection like the red light's a suggestion.

"You remember Prince?" Ezra asks, smiling a little.

"Oh my God, of *course* I remember Prince! Dude saved my ass that one time I fell out back."

Ezra rolls his eyes. "You make it sound so normal. You were climbing up the fire escape, hit your head on the ladder, and passed out."

Angel sniffed. "Why you always bringin' up *old* shit?"

"You brought it up!"

Angel waves a dismissive hand. "Whatever."

They're quiet for a little bit, but it's comfortable. *They're* quiet, but nothing else is. One of Angel's little sisters—Ezra thinks it's Elyanna—starts to cry inside the apartment. Somebody's grandmother cuts a Tahoe off down on the street, and the truck's driver is throwing out rapid-fire *fuck you*'s like he's getting paid to do it and his rent's due tomorrow. Then,

"You remember Kai?" Ezra blinks up at Angel, waits for an answer that he knows.

"Of course I remember Kai." Angel is smiling so bright, and Ezra wants to cry. "Kid was fast as hell, who runs like that? And I've never seen somebody dodge a chancla better."

Ezra had a physical for school a couple of months back, and he read something in one of those waiting room catalogs that he can't help but think about right now, while he's talking to Angel about

Prince and Brooklyn and Kai. He read that diabetes makes you more susceptible to the flu, which makes it easier for you to get pneumonia and infections just like it. Maybe missing people is a little like that too. Maybe seeing that guy at the grocery store broke a window inside him. And now that that pain's made it over all those chips of glass on the sill, it's just running up and down his veins, dipping behind his ribs. He's all sore and open now, and all those other losses are coming in, no knocking, coming in through that damn hole in his wall.

Ezra doesn't think Angel knows that the Italian soldier has anything to do with this little plan. But what he does know, knows for a fact, is that Angel would follow him anywhere. And that shit sits so heavy on his chest that he almost wants to jump out over the balcony.

But Angel would probably follow him down into the traffic, too.

They start with apartment fifty-three, where Brooklyn used to live.

"Open house in two days, huh?" Angel's thinking out loud while they're walking up the building's outdoor steps a week later.

Ezra stops walking, leans against the railing. Angel walks up a few steps before he sits down on one of them. He looks up. With the sun at his back like it is right now, Angel starts to look a lot like his name. Ezra's always liked the names he could see, the ones that have faces. *Ezra* has no face. Ezra tells Angel about the light hugging his spine.

"I know, I'm absolutely angelic. *Like* I've been telling you. Plus, even luckier for you, I have an idea."

Ezra scoffs. "Angelic. Tell me what you have in mind, *before* you get struck down."

Angel acts like he's offended. "As God already knows, and you will soon find out, it's a good plan."

And it *is* a good plan. Ezra and Angel take all the water bottles they can find, fill them up with water over and over again, do this all while their parents are at work and Angel's little sisters are too busy screaming, crying, cussing at each other to care about what the hell they're doing. Ezra and Angel walk into the empty apartment, Zephyrhills bottles tight against their stomachs, their chests, chins pushed up hard against the caps.

"You take the living room," Ezra points with his chin. "I'll take the dining room."

Angel narrows his eyes at Ezra. "Maybe I *wanted* the living room."

"So . . . what's the problem?"

"Now it's different. Now I *have* to take the living room, I can't *want it* no more."

"Dude."

Angel smiles at him all big and hops from one foot to the other, all the way over to a spot right next to one of the apartment's living room windows.

Ezra takes the dining room, like he says he will. He lets all the bottles drop out of his hands and onto the ground, and looks down at them for a bit. For some reason, it feels like the water bottles are still leaning hard and cool against his body, and the feeling doesn't go away until Ezra gets down on one knee.

He unscrews the bottles, squeezes them onto the floor until there are wet patches in the carpet, so many that he gets tired of counting. And when he's on his eighth bottle, Ezra wonders if prayers still count if you only had one knee on the ground at the time.

He goes back to the living room when he's done, watches Angel finish up.

"Which one of us knew first? Was it me or you?"

Angel turns around when Ezra asks the question.

"Hm?"

"Which one of us knew first that Brooklyn was getting kicked out, was it me or you?"

Angel thinks for a moment, squeezes the empty bottle in his hand while he does it.

"You saw the paper on the door first, right?" He finally responds.

Ezra nods, remembers. Didn't matter that the words were too small for him to read back then. Ezra knew an eviction notice when he saw one.

Ezra remembers Brook being an affectionate kid, and no amount of chickenshit playground bullying could change that about him. When he was moving out, he'd hugged him while his older brothers watched and laughed, out in front of the U-Haul. It was the first time Ezra had ever been hugged by someone that wasn't his mama, first time he'd ever been so close to a heart that didn't really beat like his.

Angel looks up at him from the ground. "Still can't believe he liked DC more than Marvel. Misguided kid, but he was still cool."

Ezra laughs. "Yeah."

He shifts from one foot to another, pumps water from the wet floor with all his moving.

❧

A few days later, when Ezra gets home from school, his mama tells him to stay away from apartment nineteen.

"Zay went in to do a check—some folks wanted to come in and look at it on Thursday, like I told you?—and the whole apartment smelled real bad. The floor was wet when he went in, and there's mold everywhere now. Mmhmm, I see that lil look in your eye. I don't want you anywhere near that place, got that?"

When Ezra doesn't say anything for a while, she puts her cup of Earl Grey down on the cracked kitchen countertop and turns around. Looks at him with eyes like damp earth, those places where things grow.

"You understand me, Ezra?"

And then he's not eating rice anymore, he's chewing sand, so many rocks rubbing up at the roof of his mouth until it's so raw that he's gonna start bleeding through his teeth if he tries to say anything, he knows it, he just knows it. As his mama is talking to him, it feels like somebody chewing Spearmint gum breathes thick across the back of his neck, and the hair at his nape is sticking out straight and hard. All he can think is *Ezra has no face, call me Zee, call me Zee . . .*

"Yes ma'am."

Her voice gets soft. "I'm your mama."

He looks down at his plate, at the center pale white like the batter head of a drum.

"Yes, mama."

Ezra comes up with the next one. They switch off planning like it's nothing, like Angel was halfway through a blink, and Ezra's just finishing it out for him, closing his eyes the rest of the way easy.

Being with Angel isn't something Ezra thinks twice about. Angel is a given, like sleep is. You get into bed and you slide down that wall you were trying to hold on to all day, into the warm dark just underneath your feet, into calm. Angel, for all of his shenanigans, is calm. Not calm the adjective, calm the noun. And, sure, Ezra can't really see anything when he slips into that warm dark, but what does he need his eyes for? He's in his bed, one leg thrown over the side, safe. Angel is safe.

If Angel had been there in the pasta aisle, Ezra doesn't think he would've seen his face on that Italian soldier.

They're on the third floor, almost at Prince's old apartment, and Angel is talking twenty miles a minute. Kid needs words like the earth needs the sun.

". . . and I *swear to God*, I don't think they sleep. Ely caught me in the kitchen last night when I was tryna steal some bananas from—but then again, is it really *stealing* if I'm taking 'em from my own kitchen? And then she was like *Angel? Is this a dream?* And I was all like *yeeeesss, now go back to sleep right now or you're gonna wake up bald in the Bahamas tomorrow.*"

Ezra's smiling. "You threatened Ely?"

"I mean is it really threatening if I'm *related* to her?"

"In what world does being related to people make stuff like that okay?"

Angel turns around when they get to Prince's door. His mouth pulls up a little, smirk just this side of mischievous.

"In every single one of them. There's some shit that don't count when your little sister or, I guess in my case, gorgeous older brother does 'em. It's like if *I* call you an asshole, versus if like, I don't know, *Nico* called you an asshole."

Ezra raises an eyebrow. "Dude, we're not related."

Angel rolls his eyes as he's opening the door. "Zee, we're a little related. Everybody here's a little related. You can't really live with people this long without getting to know them good enough to level up a lil bit."

Ezra can't decide then if he feels *stuck* or *safe* right now. Is he sweating?

Angel walks to the middle of the empty living room, starts taking off his bag. Ezra follows.

"Dude, this isn't Mario Kart."

Angel shrugs. "Good thing, too. Hate to think I'd have to stop playing just because somebody ran your ass off the road."

His voice sounds a little different to Ezra when he says that; it's like when you hear someone say one thing, but you know they're actually saying something else. If Angel's throwing his voice down a tunnel, Ezra's only catching the echoes.

Ezra sits down next to Angel while he's dumping everything out of his bag. A bunch of fruit falls out—a banana, some apples, is that a pear?—tailed by a bunch of little green toy soldiers. Ezra sighs, and he's about to say something before Angel interrupts him.

He throws his hands up. "Okay, *before* you throw me out that window, let me explain. I know you said food scraps—"

"Scraps," Ezra agrees, nods.

"But—and hear me out, this is a good one—I didn't wanna look for scraps. Last thing I need is for Ely to catch me digging through the trash. *Mamá, Angel's in the trash como una ratón.* How the hell would I live that down?"

It's Ezra's turn to roll his eyes. "No one said you had to go through the trash, dude. You coulda just snatched peels off your brothers' and sisters' plates and shit."

Angel brings a hand to his chin, thinks. "Wow, I did *not* think of that at all. But but *but*, I have an easy solution." He picks up the banana, peels it back, and starts to eat it. "I'm a boy of answers, Zee."

"Oh my God."

So they just eat some of the fruit, make it small enough to be useful. Can't really clog up a sink drain with a whole pear, Angel admits. When they're done, Angel takes the kitchen, leaves with the food scraps, and Ezra heads over to the bathroom with the toy soldiers.

He gets on his knees in front of the toilet, and when he's putting the soldiers down on the ground, he notices that the floor tile in here crisscrosses into black triangles. Was his own bathroom floor like this too? A memory cracks his present, tugs him hard into his past.

Prince was always noticing weird stuff like this, like these tiles. When Angel knocked himself out climbing the fire escape outside Ezra's room, it wasn't really all that surprising that it was Prince who found him. The kid paid attention to everything, never missed anything, and felt it like a second heartbeat whenever something was wrong. He dropped into Ezra and Angel's piece of the world the summer right before sixth grade, a few years after Brooklyn left.

Angel saw him first, just happened to spot one of the motorcycles from *Grand Theft Auto: Vice City* on his PSP screen and walked up to the kid like he'd always known him.

Because Angel makes friends just like most people bounce that one leg when they've been sitting somewhere for a long time—unconsciously, instinctively.

One time, a Saturday, when Angel was sick with the flu, Prince came over to Ezra's apartment.

Ezra opened the door, told him, "Sorry, Angel's sick," expected him to leave after that. But Prince didn't. Just looked at him with eyes so curious that Ezra started to fidget.

He'd said, "You can hang out with me when Angel's not around, too. You know that, right?"

And dammit, why'd he have to look through that stupid little opening in the fence of what Ezra said to him, spy on his truth while it sat still and lonely in the grass?

Prince could see him, peel him off Angel and really *look* at him, by himself. And it was the scariest thing, because he'd never even hung out with Brook without Angel. With Prince, he had a face, his own face.

But now, his knees are starting to hurt down here on the cold bathroom floor, and he knows that there are two other people out there somewhere running around that look just like him—some Italian soldier he's seen, and some other guy he's never known.

Ezra throws the toy soldiers into the toilet, pulls the handle down, and flushes.

☙

Angel and Ezra walk past Zay a few days later as they're going into their building and he's leaving it. He smiles at them.

And Ezra gets the sense that Zay should know about the mini tubes of All-Purpose Krazy Glue in his and Angel's pockets, almost wants to turn around himself and bring Zay to awareness, put the glue into his dazed hands without breaking eye contact.

But he doesn't, and when they're walking down a fifth-floor hallway, he's thinking of Kai so hard that he almost expects to see the kid leaning against a wall when they turn this corner.

Where the hell were you assholes?

They start in the kitchen this time. Angel throws all of his Krazy Glue onto one of the counters, and Ezra does the same.

"Zee, this is gonna be hilarious. Front door's unlocked, but every other door in here, glued shut?" Angel brings the tips of his fingers together and kisses them. "Brilliant."

Ezra laughs. "Yeah. Kid'd be proud."

"Damn straight," Angel laughs. "You remember that thing with the gazebo?"

"Of course! Saw a garden gnome when I was walking to the dollar store yesterday and I almost pissed myself."

"Evil little fuckers," Angel agrees. He pauses, leans against the counter like the remembering made him tired. "Kai was amazing."

Yeah. Kai was that feeling you get when you're standing on the roof of something, looking down at the ground and finding it insane that you were ever meant to be anywhere else but up there. The kid was vertigo, those games you used to play when you were little where you'd spin around as fast as you could with your arms thrown out, lose your balance on purpose, always know that the grass or the carpet or whatever would be there to catch you when you were out of breath and the world was still unsteady.

There's a neighborhood right behind Ezra and Angel's building with backyards like parks. It doesn't have gates, and when you're driving around the area, all the apartment complexes fall into each other, change sizes, reshape into huge two-stories whose balconies have iron arms that stretch out and open up like flowers.

Some TV show producer lives in one of the biggest houses on

that block, and a few years ago, thanks to Kai, they'd found out he has a gazebo right around back.

Ezra remembers walking down that street, Kai and Angel all excited, dancing around in anticipation like the twin baby Satans they were. Remembers seeing all those Cadillacs and feeling like the sidewalk was tipping too much to one side, like he was on a seesaw.

They went around the back of the producer's house, and Ezra and Angel got Kai over the fence, held each other by the forearms and made a lattice that the kid used to jump into the backyard. There was a little gate at the back, locked, of course, until Kai got to it. To this day Ezra still doesn't know how the kid did it, just remembers seeing these thin little sewing scissors in Kai's hand.

The gazebo was made of pretty, pale brown wood, like the thick columns that held up their building's attic. It had glass-top patio furniture, table and chairs and all, and it made Ezra feel like he'd just walked in on one of those stupid inflatable pool commercials.

Kai scoffed when they sat down at the table. "Fake house right behind the real one, imagine that. Rich people are honestly so insecure. Always need two of everything. Like damn."

Angel had said, "Yup. I might be poor, but least I'm *securely* poor."

And Kai knew that Angel was half-joking; Ezra could see it in the way the kid's mouth quirked.

But the kid leaned forward, looked Angel straight in the eye and, with a kind of heavy seriousness, said,

"Yeah."

Ezra doesn't really know why, but Angel, the same kid who'd talked his way out of two muggings and three detentions, didn't say anything back.

They sat in that gazebo for about an hour before shit hit the wall. Angel was the first to notice, saw some man with perfectly combed black hair and a tight, hard face storming over to them, tearing through the grass sky in front of the gazebo. Looking like he was about ready to grab one of them bodily and use them to beat the other two.

"Hey!" he'd yelled, as if he'd even needed to. "You all are trespassing!"

"Why's he yelling that?" Angel whispered. "Does he think we don't know?"

They were jumping over one of the sides of the gazebo when Kai was like, "Well, I got my answer."

"About . . . *what*?" Angel yelled after the kid, fighting through his panting.

Kai seemed fine though, voice incredibly even. "It's true—you can't ever *not* talk."

By then, Angel was panting way too hard to rage like he wanted to at Kai's disrespect.

Ezra had never run so hard in his life, not before, and never since. His lungs felt like they were gonna dissolve inside his chest. The fence kept getting farther and farther away from them. When the man started throwing garden gnomes, bearded little clay assholes wheeling just past their heads, they were at the gate. Kai, who'd outrun them, made it to the fence a little earlier, held the gate open, waited for them to run through.

Then the kid locked it behind them, and they ran and ran and ran, even when they realized they could stop.

Ezra remembers everything that happened after that even more clearly.

They were in the parking lot, trying to catch their breaths (well, Angel and Ezra anyway), hands on their knees. Angel's mom, whose voice has an unbelievable range, yelled down from their apartment window for him to *ven acá, chico! Right now!* And Angel was sulking, tired, breathing hard, but he went.

When Ezra was finished catching his breath, he looked up at Kai, hands still on his knees. Was the kid even sweating? Face completely dry, *Teen Titans* shirt unwrinkled. The only thing that gave Kai away, told anyone who might care enough to look this closely a little bit about what'd just happened to them, was the kid's hair. It was pushed to one side, heavy over a single ear, coily pieces sticking up wherever they felt like it.

Kai laughed. "You good?"

Ezra remembers laughing too, being like, "Yeah, no sweat."

They were walking into the building, just rounding the corner right next to the elevator when Kai pulled Ezra into the tiny alcove right next to the vending machines.

The kid kissed him, and Ezra kind of felt like he does when the wind's blowing hard, almost too hard, and he's breathing against it. Sure, it takes a little getting used to, but soon his body realizes that it's the same air, just moving a little faster, and takes it in just like it does when the atmosphere is standing still. And when that kid kissed him, he felt like he was made of something beautifully, painfully solid.

Kai took some getting used to, forced him to crank his tolerance dial for *ridiculous shit* up by like sixty. He didn't find himself falling into Kai like he did with Angel. He was falling *with* the kid, and damn if that didn't feel a little better.

"I miss that kid." Angel brings him back to the late afternoon quiet of Kai's old kitchen.

"Yeah," Ezra jumps up onto the counter, sits there with his head up against the cabinets behind him. "Yeah, me too."

"Angel?" Ezra swallows, waits for him to respond.

Angel looks up. He's sitting on the ground now. One of the Krazy Glue tubes falls off the counter, and he catches it. Holds on to it, turns it over in his hands like it's the most interesting thing he's ever seen.

"It's completely like we're related, dude."

Angel's eyebrows come together, that confusion that Ezra doesn't like very much comes back.

"What do you mean?"

"You know so much about me . . ." Ezra thinks about his mom in the kitchen that day, looking at him like she understood.

Angel laughs, looks away. Says all quiet, almost so low that Ezra doesn't hear it over the ceiling fan's humming, "You're easy to figure out. Kai was like that, too. You guys were like the same person."

Then, he looks up again, smiles. "Zee, you know something? That dude at the grocery store got me thinkin'. I always thought you really looked like your mom. First time I saw y'all together, I was like *yup, that's her kid, cut copy and freaking paste.* But then I was like, sure, they look alike, but his chin's weird. Can you believe that? I was so freaking insane. I was like, nah, that chin's all his."

Ezra's heart is a neutron star behind the sticks of his ribs, hot and tight, moving this time, beating so fast that he doesn't think he could ever fall into that warm dark calm with a pulse like this. Angel's doing the peeling now, not Prince, dragging him right off his skin, forcing him to remember what it feels like to have his own body.

Ezra lays down on the countertop, ignores the tubes of glue as they fall on the ground next to Angel. One of Ezra's arms is just hanging off the side of the counter. He hits Angel's cheek, but the kid doesn't react to it.

Ezra looks up at the ceiling fan, stares at it so long that his eyes start to water. But he starts to feel like something inside him is finally gonna cool down. Finally.

He just wants to stop burning.

Wynwood

I always remind people of other people. I'm used to it by now, having somebody else borrow my face for a little while. 'Cause I'm that hard thing people throw their memories against. I'm what they bounce off of right before they cut through the air and get back to who they really belong to. Before they section that sheet of atoms draped between us, rip apart that fabric wall till the strips are laying down at our feet like leaves. Till we're just staring at each other across that gaping throat the tear makes.

It happens after five but before seven. You know, when the sun's dripping down the sky, brazed orange up against a growing darkness. The fading sunlight slinks through the space around it until both things find themselves inside of each other, figure out they can make the softest purple so they do. It's not dark yet and I'm two blocks away from home. Maybe it's three. I usually cut through the empty lot right behind the beauty supply store on Sixth. The chain-link fence runs parallel to the lot.

There's a hole in the fence that leads pretty beautifully right up to my street. All I have to do is walk across the concrete partition that leads across the canal and I'm golden. I almost drowned in that canal once. And I know that every time I cross it, it feels like my lungs are full of water again, like my own panic's got its arms wrapped around my chest again.

Nico pulled me out, dragged me onto the barren narrow bank. And when I opened my eyes, coughing, all I could think about was how his head cut against the glass blue sky like a fucking sun. And if I thought that I kind of liked the way his eyes got all big and scared for me, kind of liked how their pretty green made me think about Saturday mornings in the grass behind my grandma's backyard, well . . . nobody needed to know that.

I'd seen him sometimes in the cafeteria, with the other Colombian kids, but having somebody drag you out of a canal? It changes things, makes you close. So when I started going everywhere with Nico, walking to school with him, going home with him, playing with him on the weekends . . . people didn't think I was gay, they thought I was grateful. Shit, I ran with it.

I think he knew. Before I even told him, I think he—

I'm crossing the street in front of the post office and a royal blue Chevy Tahoe misses me by like half a foot. My heart falls through my ribcage, into my stomach. Stays there long after the truck's gone. I'd always thought that there had to be an easier way to let everybody know how far along you were in your midlife crisis, but trucks seem to be the way to go down here. Cars have already started to swerve around me by the time I start to get out of the street.

I'm almost there. I can see the Family Dollar up ahead, so I'm less than a block away from the beauty supply shop.

I always love visiting my grandma (not the Cuban one that hates me; the Black one that hates my mom) in Wynwood. She's just a city over, not that far, so I walk. I go for her, stay for the art, the streets of murals, that kind of shit that would make white classicists pass the fuck out. With her there's this love inside a four-bedroom ranch-style that wraps around me, leaves me warm for days on end. Then I get the walls of screaming colors, stark blues and greens and yellows and pinks and oranges and reds yelling just to yell just to yell. Screaming and screaming and screaming at me until something inside me picks up the key and starts giving as good as it gets.

Liberty City's where my heart got built, where it learned to pump blood through me, where it's probably gonna stay. But Wynwood? Wynwood makes my soul shake something fucking awful inside me, so hard my teeth rattle. Makes my soul want to take over, turn my body into an afterthought, into postscript.

I think my mom can see it sometimes when I come home, maybe. My soul leaving and my heart staying and me, caught up in the middle not choosing. Less because I can't and more because I don't want to have to.

My mom hates her mom just as much as my grandma hates her. Think maybe it has something to do with when she got pregnant with me. My mom sees my grandma in me, Wynwood in me, and I think she loves me harder because she's trying to get rid of both. Trying to Clorox that shit right out of me with her sacrifice, her twelve-hour nursing shifts at Jackson Memorial, the bikes, the phones, the skateboards, the clothes the clothes the clothes, the jackets, the jeans, the shirts, the bags. Tommy Hilfiger would want to marry her on the spot if he could see my fucking closet.

I think that's when it started, this vicious thing between them— when I was inside my mom, asleep, unborn. When I was inside her and my grandma found out that my dad was white (no, not just white. Cuban. Worse). When my grandma saw her past, laid out in front of her. Years and years and years of hearing *nigger negro sucio mono*, of being spit on, of avoiding Little Havana like the plague came back and picked up a mortgage there.

So growing up I always felt it. But here's the thing—my mom and grandma hated each other but my mom would never keep me from her. That's the thing with my family—we're loyal to each other, even when we don't like each other. Loyalty drinks up the hate, grows strong on all that bad blood.

My grandma was the first person to let me know I remind people of other people. I was six. I was at my grandma's house and she called me into the kitchen. But she said Jasmine, my mom's name. I stood there, kitchen island barely coming up to my chin. I stared up at her. She stared down at me. It took her so long to realize what she'd said. And that wasn't the last time it happened, either. Still happens. On this visit I was sketching at the dining room table and she walked up behind me, wrapped an arm around my shoulders and said *whatcha workin' on, Jazz?*

I'm pretty sure my grandma loves me. But I also think that some of that love she's holding for me, wherever she's keeping it, is meant for my mom. She can't give it to her, won't let herself. So she gives it to me. I hold it in my pockets, my bookbag, between the sheets in my sketchbook, in my socks, my shoes. But I take it all out on my mom's front porch. Think it would hurt her too much if I came into the house with it.

My mom was the second. And she gave me a two-for-two, bless her heart.

I was nine. I was just playing in the backyard. Hadn't met Nico yet. Kwame and Tyler were both visiting family out of state. I didn't really like any of the other kids in the neighborhood enough to invite them over (sue me). I don't know what the fuck I was doing. You know how boredom brews up inside a nine-year-old, makes them do the most mundane, ridiculous shit to tamp it down. I was running back and forth across our tiny backyard, trying to figure out how fast I could really go. Back. Forth. Back. Forth. Big palm tree. Propane tank. Big palm tree. Propane tank.

I tripped, and my knee fell hard against a sharp ass rock. I was mostly in shock then, but now that I think about it, I was bleeding pretty bad. Red blood ran under the grit and gravel on brown skin. Thought I looked a little like a National Geographic volcano, hot lava dribbling out of me, eating up all the trees on my expanse.

I didn't cry and I didn't yell or anything. I don't think my mom would've found me outside if she hadn't been walking past the patio door just as I fell. She ran out and fell to her knees, looked at my cut. She hugged me. When she pulled back to ask me how I felt, if I had any pain, her eyes were wet. I told her I was fine.

"Juanlu, don't lie to me."

We stared at each other, hot lava between us. She bit her lip when she realized what she'd said, but she didn't correct herself. Wonder what she thought would happen, if she went back and fixed it. So that's how I figured out my dad's name. Juanlu. Juan Luis.

When she came back outside with the hydrogen peroxide she gave me a look too big for me and her tears came harder. I think she was seeing my grandma, what they used to be. Maybe those times when my mom fell and busted her ass playing, and grandma came out with that brown bottle. When grandma used to run out and check up on her. I wonder if grandma was serious with it, face folded up with worry. I wonder if she tried to make my mom laugh.

I think when she looked at me that day on the ground in our backyard, the past cut her up. Carved her into pieces it took for itself. Left her raw and open, blood splattered all over the present. The life that came first, with my grandma. The one that came after, with my dad.

But *God* I think too much. Nico's right.

"You gotta stop that shit, babe," he's always telling me. "Your face *screams* 'come fuck with me.'"

I love my mom and I love my grandma, but they take pieces of me for themselves, reach through me and around me and across me towards each other.

Nico doesn't divide me like that. He keeps me whole when he looks at me, talks to me. I can only ever remind him of me, I think. I mean, how many people has he pulled out of a polluted Florida waterway?

And like a goddamn prophet, that shit Nico's always telling me about how I look way too off my guard when I'm walking through the street? Comes to pass. His warnings find footing.

I'm passing by the bus stop. Street's empty. The cars running past on the street make the only noise for miles. Makes sense. Sundays are always quiet like this, slow. We have way too many churches down here for us not to respect God at least a little. And in a place where nobody can ever keep still for too long, silence is the highest praise.

Out of the corner of my eye I see some kid in a blue plaid sweatshirt texting on his phone, standing under the bus stop lamps, that white light caked in blue. Another kid's sitting on the hard plastic bench, headphones in, head down.

The thing about reminding people of other people is that it's a complete shot in the dark. I've gotten quick smiles at the Publix, right before the lady with the sew-in wig realizes I'm not her son. Soft casual *where were you?*s at the Steak 'n Shake from pretty girls who register I'm not their boyfriend only after a few blinks. But I've also gotten tight lips and raised brows from cashiers at the Wingstop (I like their ranch better than Wings on Fire's) who realize I'm not their ex or the guy that cut them off while they were getting off the I or that dude who walked into class without holding the door for them only after they *really look* at my face.

I'm almost past the bus stop when the kid in the plaid walks up to me, ditches my periphery for my direct field of vision. I'm just starting to think *you want the shoes, right?* when he punches me in the face.

I'm gonna spare you the poetry. Getting punched in the face isn't like anything else in this entire fucking world. Newton's bitch ass says that for every action there's an equal and opposite reaction. Every hit gets a hit back. But *damn* if it isn't the shittiest thing in the world when that's the only thing I can hope for, that my face fractures Blue Plaid's knuckles a little bit.

I'm laying down on my back on the sidewalk now, staring up at the world's ceiling getting dark. I move to get up. Somebody kicks me in the ribs, evicts the breath from my chest. Try to curl up on my side and what's that shit Nico's always telling me about getting jumped? Protect the head. I move to cover my head with my arms but somebody jerks me to my feet. Somebody pulled back and kicked the world as hard as they could—that's why it's spinning like this. Someone's holding my arms pinned behind my back. Must be Blue Plaid, because Headphones is standing in front of me now, looking at me with an anger that sears my throat raw. He hits me in the stomach and I wanna double over, fold in half, but I can't.

"You hard now, motherfucker? Huh?" Headphones is asking me, voice all warbly like it's coming through water.

And all I can think right now is *who do you see who do you see who the fuck do you see*. I try to say something but Headphones hits me again and I don't get the chance. I try harder.

"Mother . . . fucker, I'm not . . . I'm not . . ." I push my words through the empty space that cuts through the forest of pain growing inside me. Between the branches behind my face. Between the leaves in my chest.

And I see it, clear as anything. When Headphones realizes I'm not whoever the fuck he wanted. He looks at me, eyes wide, anger gone. And he says,

"Oh shit. Ooooh shit. P, it's not him!"

Blue Plaid drops me. I land on my front, break my fall with my arm. When I look up they're running into the sun. Good. I hope it eats them the fuck up.

I don't know how long I'm lying there. Street's still empty and I'm thinking of course this shit had to happen on the quietest Sunday in Miami history. I'm trying to take inventory. Face? Right cheek hurts like hell, pain in the dairy section, right next to the yogurt. Ribs? Hurt less, ache with the produce, between the tomatoes. Think Blue Plaid's shoe had a soft toe. Think they were Champions or something. Stomach? Hurts less than the cheek but more than the ribs, pang with the cereal but not the good shit. No Cinnamon Toast Crunch or Cocoa Puffs or Cookie Crisps. It's with the muesli, the plain oats, the unsweetened Cheerios.

I roll over to my side, the one with the uninjured ribs, and I cough. When I look down at the concrete I'm relieved to find that there's no blood. A good sign. My arms feel a little strained from

Blue Plaid holding them so tight behind my back, but they're okay I think. I use them to brace myself, and I get up.

I limp over to the bus stop bench, sit down heavier than I intended to and pay for it with my ribs telling me to fuck off. I wince as I pull out my phone, go to call my mom. I pause over her name, her contact picture where she's smiling big in front of the Dolphin Mall, browner with the summer. I'm in it too. Her arms are tight around me. I'm smiling softer but fuck, I look so fucking happy. I think about limping home, coming into the house with a huge bruise on my face while she's getting ready to go to work. I know what she would see. Her baby got jumped her mom got jumped the love of her damn life got jumped on the street while he she he was walking home. I breathe deep, and the breath sidles up to my bruised ribs, swats at them on its way out my chest.

I lock my phone and slip it into my pocket. I get up. The neon lights of the beauty supply store are shining back at me. I can see the start of the chain-link fence right behind the building, even from the bus stop. I put up the hood of my jacket and walk the other way.

Nico lives right next to the Dollar General on Sixty-Fifth, in the neighborhood with the water tower. It sounds stupid but when I was little I thought that was the coolest shit ever. Growing up down here, one of the first things you learn is that the tap water's probably gonna give you nerve damage (not saying that it *will*, just saying that it *might*). Thought it was the coolest thing ever that Nico lived right under something we needed so bad.

It scared me shitless when I figured out I looked like myself to him. It made me want to run into a Publix and dance down the aisles but it also scared me shitless. I was eight and I felt naked, like he could see everything. God.

We were sitting on the floor in his room, playing *GTA: San Andreas*. He looked over at me, head tilted to the side a little, and said,

"You have a bunch of dots on your face. So does my mami, but she calls them beauty marks. But we're boys, so what do we call them?"

I didn't want to look him in the eye then. I wanted to look at the TV screen, where CJ was paused in the middle of throwing somebody out of an El Dorado. But it felt like Nico's eyes would be wherever I looked, so I shrugged and joked,

"Do they make me ugly?"

Nico shook his head, all serious, and the air around me got so tight that I had to unpause GTA with my controller, to turn it back into something I could breathe.

When I get to his house the driveway's empty. His parents must be at work. Luz is probably at her boyfriend's. Abril might be at a sleepover.

I climb the steps of his porch with some difficulty, ignore the doorbell, knock hard right on the door. His front door's got that frosted glass that looks good but doesn't actually let you see shit. Wonder what I'd look like to him right now, hazy body mixed up with the indistinct light of the streetlamps. He takes too long to answer. I knock again. I hear footsteps now, and the door opens so fast it makes me dizzy.

"Dude, why the fuck are you knocking on my door like you pay this damn mortgage—"

I look up and he stops talking.

"Holy shit." He steps aside. "What the fuck are you doing out here? Come inside."

I move to come inside, but my foot catches on the threshold and I trip. Nico catches me, wraps my arm around his neck and helps me to the living room.

I stare at the dark screen of the turned-off TV. The house is quiet. Nico's moving around the kitchen. I hear the freezer door slam, and a few moments later he's back, handing an ice pack to me before he sits down in the armchair to my right. I hold the pack to my cheek and feel instant relief run through me.

"What the fuck happened?" he asked, the calmest I've ever heard him.

I look up. His voice worries me. That calm's hard and hot, like iron left to smolder. That harshness like searing burning broken glass, that ferocity that tells me someone's gonna get fucked up no matter what I say. And in moments like these the truth and the lie have the same damn face, so why bother.

"Got jumped. They thought I was somebody else."

I see his fists clench in the light coming in from the kitchen. "Hijo de *puta.*"

I hold the ice pack tighter against my face.

"Where?"

"The bus stop in front of the Family Dollar."

"Who?"

"Probably some South Beach kids. I've never seen them around here before."

"And you won't see them around here again."

"Nico . . ."

"Fucking comemierdas think they can just run around here and fuck up whoever or whatever the fuck they—"

"Nico . . ."

"—I mean are they fucking kidding? You see somebody on the street and you just—"

"Nico . . ."

"But it's not gonna be no two-bit mistaken identity *Face/Off* Nicholas Cage bullshit when *we*—"

"Nico, can I stay here tonight?"

He calms down when he looks up at me, for real this time. I wrap his anger up in a gentleness I thought somebody kicked out of me at a bus stop in front of a Family Dollar. I give that anger nowhere to go. And he says,

"Yes."

My mom should just be clocking in right now. I text her from

Nico's bathroom, tell her where I am. I look at myself in the mirror. I want to see just how bad shit is.

And it's . . . pretty bad, but I'd say that for getting hit super hard in the face with a closed fist . . . maybe not as bad as it could be.

A bruise grows from the corner of my left eye to the brown shore a few miles right below my left cheekbone, its own little continent. It's a pretty deep purple and it's gonna get worse before it gets better but I think I might be able to work something out with Luz, get her to let me borrow some of her concealer. I can YouTube it before I get home if her generosity ends with just lending me the concealer, figure out how the fuck to use it.

Nico's standing in the hallway when I get out of the bathroom, waiting for me.

"If you want, you can sleep in Abril's room, in a bed. She's at Sloan's."

I want to sleep in Nico's room, in his bed, but it happened again. Somebody turned me into someone else, and I got my ass beat for it. I feel loose, unmoored, like I got sent back to that blank space we're in before God calls us in. Before we're anything.

"Abril's room sounds good. I'm starting to like pastels."

The smile that Nico tries to give me loses its way to his eyes. He runs a hand through his hair, like he was gonna try to touch me but I burn too hot. He never knows what to do when I get like this. He described it to me once. Said it's like taking a tire iron to plexiglass.

I try to fall asleep, I really do. Roll around in Abril's princess twin as much as my ribs and my stomach will let me. But trying to sleep with fresh injuries has to be the ninth circle of hell. That's what Satan decides you have to do for the rest of forever, when you get down there. Whenever I get close to something like sleep the ache in my stomach or my chest or my face yanks me back, slaps me awake to the dark that's sitting like a slab of concrete on my chest right now and *fuck* maybe I was wrong maybe my ribs *are* broken and the shards caught a lung and that's why I can't breathe right now I can't breathe I can't breathe I can't breathe—

I sit up. A tabby kitten on the giant poster opposite the bed stares back at me with huge marble eyes. I leave the room.

My ribs still hurt like hell, face still sore as shit. But I came here 'cause I breathe the best with him, right? Damn if it doesn't sit on my chest, knowing that neither my mom nor my grandma really knows how to give me a life that's just my own. One that I don't have to share with all the people waiting out inside their pasts. I don't want to have to carry breaths that aren't my own.

Through the windows in the hallway I can see the driveway. I don't know what time it is but it must still be pretty early. No one's home yet.

I push open the door to Nico's room, and I can hear him snoring quietly. He's facing the door, mouth wide open, curls wrapping around his face like dark vines. I walk over and nudge his shoulder. Nico's always been a light sleeper and he wakes up immediately, eyes misty with sleep.

"Asaad?" he croaks. "You good?"

He always says something like this before we start, no matter how many times we do it. No matter where it happens.

I don't say anything. I nod but I don't think he sees it. I don't know, maybe he does. Either way, I answer: I pull back his sheets and climb on top of him, my knees up against his waist, the length of my calves up against his hips.

He's shirtless. I put my hands on his chest, palms prickling with the feeling of his heart beating steady inside him. He's fully awake now but his face still has that muted sleepy calm that only ever comes out at night. He's holding my hips now. The moon swings through the window to interrupt the dark around us and for a second it looks like my hands and his chest are a single thing. Like I dipped my hands into a pool the same color as me, like my fingers grew a chest, like they painted us conjoined, a Wynwood vista. And it's here, on top of him, that I start having a really shitty thought. Maybe I'm wrong, maybe I don't actually have my own face for him. Anyone, Nico would've pulled anyone from that canal—

But I don't know how to ask him about something like that so I don't. I take off my hoodie and we make the softest purple.

Muscle Memory

It starts with an Old Spanish–style on Cordova. We're heading over to the Checkers a few blocks away, and we're walking down Jefferson, about to hit the Western Union on Ridge. There's a tinfoil sky hanging over us.

When the days are gray like this it always makes me nervous as hell. Gray doesn't take any sides, it's neutral. And on days like this it feels like everything else is trying to make up for that, trying to make itself extra special. It's all moving faster. Nothing has any soft lines anymore, no sluggishness, and I'm looking at a world distilled. Cars with solar flare paint, buildings with razor blade corners, trees and grass and bushes with radioactive leaves. Shining with that bright green shit they need gloves and special suits to handle, energy irrepressible.

Makai's walking up ahead of me and I can barely keep up. He fell out of an animated feature, edges refined, skin that kind of brown no one's ever gonna come up with a good name for. You'd find it in the woods, maybe, if you spent enough time looking. Maybe you'd see it if the earth got sick and its skin got thinner, and the hot gold magma inside its veins brushed up against the dirt you're standing on. See how the colors run into each other, climb across one another, slot into each other to make something you still can't name, something that sears any commentary to the back of your throat and closes your mouth shut. Makai's like that. Inexplicable.

And inside the capsule of the bright fast day, he's the brightest fastest thing for miles. You ever met anyone like that? Those people you feel like you can never really get a good look at—they're moving too quick, you can't see them anymore, dammit, you blinked and now they're gone—but fuck it all to hell, you're gonna try anyway?

We're walking past the Western Union logo when he says it.

"We're really gonna be the only ones not going to Lion Country with everybody else? This is some bullshit."

I nod. "Yeah, it's fucked."

"It's like we never get to do anything. Everything costs money, everything has a fucking age restriction."

When Mrs. Richardson told us how much Lion Country's entry fee was, Makai and I were devastated. Looking at our faces you would've thought we'd just gotten laid off after twenty years of dedicated, back-breaking work.

Everyone else was going. Of course they were. Our parents loved the idea of having us go to the better uptown school, but I don't think they thought it through. Don't think they ever really considered it. How lonely we'd be.

We're walking past the bus stop now. Some guy older than my dad stares at Makai, tracks him with his eyes. I move up to Makai's left, block him from the guy's view.

"And are we even *technically* done with eighth grade if we don't go? Like yeah, we'll be in high school next year or whatever, but we still missed a huge part of what makes our last middle school year bomb."

I see King's Creek across the street, and I watch a big Lincoln drive through the gates. I don't even notice that I've stopped walking until Makai's nudging my shoulder.

"Leto? Leto, what's—"

He cuts himself off. I don't think the silver Lincoln turning into King's Creek expected an audience today. The old guy driving it gives us a weird look. He barely gives the gates enough time to open.

"Hmm."

When I look over at Makai, there's a little smile on his face. Small enough to miss if you're not looking hard enough. He had it that

Thursday last year, when he asked Ms. Henderson to use the bathroom. After lunch that day everybody went back to class, but most of our teachers weren't there. Turns out the knob on the teacher's lounge door stuck. We got an extra free period right then while our janitors tried to figure out how the hell to fix it.

Had it when the lady who lives in the modern-style five-bedroom up the street from our complex woke up bald the morning after she hit me with her Lexus and drove off.

Had it right before he broke his arm walking up our landlord's driveway, a few weeks after she tried to have him and his family evicted.

I narrow my eyes at him, suspicious. "What?"

He shrugs, noncommittal. "How badly do you wanna go to Lion Country?"

And I think about it. I really have to think about it, because whatever Makai's about to suggest . . . it's gonna need everything from me, no space for doubt.

The gray's almost completely gone now, leaves the sky a chalky blue. I'm looking out at the side of the street we're standing on, out at the cracked asphalt stretching out in front of us like an imperfect ocean. The chain-link fences like gray nets around our houses, our strip malls of thirsty concrete, trees that always feel like they're trying to run out of your eyeline. Some place with no intensity, some place color forgot, where hue dripped through its scrawny fingers and rainbow droplets found each other in the gutter, raced each other to the sewer.

And I think about seeing the lions and the giraffes and the sloths and the birds for real. Living, breathing things that aren't people sad or people desperate or people disgusted or people lost confused ~~lonely~~, about seeing what grass looks like when it's everywhere and when it's not fighting for attention, and my answer's *badly. Really, really badly.* How could it be anything else?

"Bad." I say it out loud. Makai nods.

We go home that day, sit in my room and come up with a plan. The money and the permission slips for Lion Country are due on Monday, so whatever we're about to do, it's gotta be quick.

"It can't be King's, too much security. What about Verdant Oaks?"

I shake my head. "No. We might get through the gates, but there's always a patrol car rolling around."

"Hmm, Hardwood, then? It's far but we could probably make it?"

"What about one of the houses on Cordova?"

He smiles big. "Yes. Oh my fucking God, *yes!* We really shouldn't have jumped straight to gated communities when—Okay, okay, this could work. Fuck, okay."

Our plan is a non-plan. I sleep over at Makai's because his apartment complex is closer to Cordova. It's right across the street from that corner where Sherman Avenue turns into it. We stay up past midnight, wait till Makai's parents and little sisters are all asleep. Then we slip out into the streets heavy with the nighttime quiet.

I stare at the back of Makai's neck while we walk, where one of his braids curls up against his nape and makes its own little galaxy.

We're so nervous we go with the first upscale house we see. Old Spanish design. Walls a loud yellow quiet with the dark. Brown roof. One story. Perfect lawn. There aren't any cars in the driveway. There's a gate right next to the house that probably leads to the backyard. Makai and I pad up to it and it's—not locked. We look at each other while we're standing on the other side of the gate, in that backyard. Share a single breath, feel thrill chasing down anxiety inside our chests.

The back door's not locked either. It's one of the sliding glass ones, the ones white people can't seem to stop walking into in those Windex commercials.

I thought it would feel different, walking into one of these houses. Didn't think they'd look lived-in, didn't expect the rainbow blanket hanging off the back of the bright white sofa. The Blu-ray DVDs on the coffee table, sliding off each other, like somebody threw them down and forgot about them because they could. Because they're home and they can do shit like that here. Wasn't ready to see the family pictures. The dad's tall and tan, the mom's a little taller than him, and the kids are cute as hell. They're at the beach and they're all smiling—

"Um, Leto?" Makai whispers. "Can we do this little open-house walk-through some *other* time?"

We grab the first kinda-fancy things we see, these two vases on the tiny table next to the loveseat. They're white, and they have blue vines that wrap around them like fingers. And they're so pretty I almost want to keep them.

We pawn them the next day, and the guy at the counter raises his eyebrows at us. Makai gives him his bomb-diffusing grin while I try on my best poker face.

One day and sixty dollars later, we're riding around in a safari jeep, watching a grown giraffe and its baby walk across the green. It's like somebody tore my life right open, let me see all the things dancing around behind it. And it makes my blood sing, turns it into a five-octave powerhouse. I'm dizzy with the feeling, giddy with it, fucking elated with it.

It's supposed to be a one-off thing, but it's not. Every time Makai needs money for something, we do a house. A physical for school, a trip to Universal with his band, a light bill. We never plan shit out, never know exactly how we're gonna get into the houses or what we're gonna take, but we get better at it. It's like muscle memory.

And me? I get some of the money too. I pay for shit with it. Stuff at school, bills at home. But every single house we do gives me a glimpse of shit I've never been a part of. Families where everybody gets their own room, where expenses are an afterthought, where everybody's in every single picture and everybody looks happy. Sometimes I'll look over at Makai while we're in some sleek King's Creek kitchen and I'll just see him staring at the coffee maker, the sub-zero fridge, the food processor, and I'll feel whatever he's feeling so hard my breath's unsteady with it. It's that longing, that wanting, yeah, that wistfulness. You might call it jealousy but I call it something else. It's looking out at all the worlds out there, watching them all spread out in front of you, and knowing you got one of the worst ones. And that's not an ache I could ever explain to anybody who's never felt it.

When I was younger, before Makai, I would dream myself to pieces, shards of me like lava glass on the cracked streets inside my head. And every time I tried to pick up those bits of my splintered self they would cut at my fingers until red danced so angry and so beautiful on my skin that I felt like a dying sun. I felt like the tiny, malnourished strip of the universe that God had given me was falling apart, losing itself.

Makai? He never told me but I knew when I met him that he felt like that too. And knowing that made shit easier.

It hurts to see all the better lives that you didn't get, the off-limit ones, strung out in front of you. But with every single thing we take from those houses, the vases, the china, the glasses, it feels like we're chipping away at worlds with no room for us. We're building moments with them.

And it makes things better for a little while.

July in New Orleans

Death has dimples.

Pocket sees them from his booth when Death walks in, tall and lean and easy as summer, catches them as an old mouth smiles out of a young brown face. The girl behind the cash register, suddenly shyer than Pocket remembers her being when he first got here, takes his order, and Death's eyes find his as he turns around to search for a seat. He smiles at Pocket too, quirks his lips all friendly to break the tension, like you're supposed to do with strangers who are supposed to stay strangers.

Pocket isn't fooled. If he was anyone else, maybe he would be. But he had been taught, by generations of fierce, stormy, hurricane women, that to really know a person, you have to look at their mouth. The go-to for most is the eyes, but eyes are too volatile, too fickle. Eyes are for the nowness of emotion, for things that you feel in minutes or seconds. Mouths are for what you feel in days, weeks, years.

Understanding too wide for words settles in his stomach as he looks at the curve of that mouth. Some of that understanding, Pocket thinks, dribbles through the smile that he gives in return, because Death falters. His smile turns tight, and he puts a few booths between them when he takes his seat. Pocket wants to laugh.

Pocket sees the mint corner of a ten-dollar bill peeking out from underneath one of the sticky brochures on Death's table as he escapes the diner. Pocket grabs his bag and follows. He catches the man out in the parking lot, before he can leave.

Death sees him as he walks up to his car, and he rolls down his window with a worn sigh.

"Look, I know I look like 'somebody' to everybody. I just have one of those faces, you know?"

Pocket admits that this much is true. Looking at Death's face makes the back of his mind itchy, like a memory is trying to tiptoe its way into the scope of his awareness. Death could be a second cousin that he played with once at his grandmama's house. He could be a friend he had once in elementary school. He could be someone he kissed when he was little.

Pocket laughs. "Nah, man. You've got it all wrong. I recognized you as soon as I saw you. Though if you were gonna show up Black, I was expecting a bit more James Earl Jones and less Lenny Kravitz."

"You talk to every stranger like this?"

"You're not a stranger."

Death studies him hard, and Pocket feebly recalls that he should be scared. But fear runs away from him, and he's too puzzled to chase it.

"I have to go," Death tells him.

"And I have to leave," Pocket responds.

"What's your name?" Death asks.

Pocket is leaning against the passenger-side door with his elbow on the pane and his fist against his cheek, and he turns to look at Death when he speaks.

"Pocket."

Death raises a brow. "Your actual name."

"My actual name doesn't matter. They treat me like the one they gave me."

Pocket has a deep, dark birthmark the size of a shot glass and the shape of a shovel over his sternum, has had it since he was a baby. But Pocket is the only one who thinks it looks like a shovel—to everyone else, it was, and is, a pocket. That was the outside story, the one that went down easy. The one that would crack your teeth was that for as long as he has been alive, Pocket has belonged to everybody else. Everyone he knows tucks the things that they don't want to lose away in him, like what they want the future to look like, or what they hope to have when that inscrutable time rolls around. Like his mama, when she thought he could replace his daddy. Like Kay, when she thought he could replace hers.

But the thing with being a pocket is that not everything you're given is for safekeeping. You're also given the things that people don't want to see anymore, like what they're afraid of, or what they can't do. His mama tried to give him the fear his daddy left in his place, tried to wrap it around his neck like a too-tight scarf. Kay tried to give him the shame she felt when he wouldn't, or couldn't, (but honestly, they were the same to him) be with her how she wanted, tried to buckle it around his waist like a belt with no holes. Dee tried to give him his rage when Pocket didn't want to be loved the way he thought he oughta be—in secret, in the dark, tried to pour it down his throat like something burning and nasty, like Everclear with sawdust in it.

Pocket tells Death this, tells him everything, unabridged and achingly honest.

Death is silent for a little while, looks out at the long stretch of highway in front of him in deep thought, with single-minded concentration, like he isn't the last person in the car who should be worried about a crash.

"You running away then?" Death asks finally.

"More like a brisk walk in the other direction."

Death laughs, and Pocket feels weirdly gratified. "Good. Least you're leaving because you want to."

Pocket looks at him, at his mouth, and finds some sadness sitting shoulder to shoulder with the oldness.

"Who did you lose?"

Death laughs again. "I don't have to point out to you how ironic that is, right?"

Pocket grins. "Death has a sense of humor. Who knew?"

"Can't be all doom and gloom all the time. I'd bore myself."

"Can't think of anything more boring," Pocket agrees.

Death returns Pocket's wry smile.

"I'm looking for a girl." Pocket raises his eyebrow at how Death's voice halts just a little bit on *girl*. "She's nothing like me."

"What's she like then?"

"You know that short little while between living and dying? You know, when you're not quite dead but you're not all that alive?"

"Like when you're near death."

"Yeah," Death agrees, his eyes twinkling, "when you're near death. She's like that."

"Bro, if I wasn't like 100 percent sure you're being completely literal right now, that would be either the best compliment or worst insult I've ever heard somebody give their girl." Pocket gives his inflection a little hitch as he ends on *girl*, just like Death had, just to see what he'll do.

Death shrugs amusedly, and looks at Pocket out of the corner of his black, black eye. He picks up on the hitch.

"She's gone now, and I have to go find her. Well, I've already found her—I know where she is. I have to go get her."

"How'd you lose her?"

And Death tells him. He tells this skinny boy with the child's nose and the big deer eyes, the first human being to ever recognize him (well, since Caesar, but his presence in the room had been too obvious then, so he didn't really count that one), about how he lost her. Him. However they were choosing to manifest right about now.

"People like to see life and death as a dichotomy, and that's perfectly fine. Just perfectly wrong. Fact is, death is life when it closes, and they really shouldn't be thought of as all that different. But

Near Death makes everything make a little more sense. She keeps things fluid. She's our intermediary."

"What does that have to do with her going missing?"

Death lets out a frustrated little laugh. "Someone came back from the dead. Dammit, I can't believe that ritual down in Viñales actually worked—"

"Why does that matter?"

"You've cut off the very incarnation of death *twice* now."

"Death's incarnation needs to stop getting sidetracked."

Death rolls his eyes. "Coming back from the dead . . . that's really the furthest you can get from being close to death. The two are mutually exclusive. We're always together, and we have to be— natural law and all that—but every time a resurrection happens, she gets hurt. She gets taken away from me, and she's dropped some random place."

Pocket's eyes light up excitedly. *What a curious child*, Death thinks without bite.

"This the first time this has happened?"

"The second. I've had pretty mixed feelings about Palestine since the first time."

"Holy crap."

"Exactly."

Pocket goes silent for a moment, and Death is so startled by it that after a while, he looks over at the kid. Pocket is smiling when he does, and he's looking ahead at the road like he's the one driving.

"Where are they this time?" he asks.

"New Orleans."

"What's their name?" he asks.

"July."

"July?"

"July."

Pocket laughs. "July in New Orleans."

belly

When she disappears on purpose, Auntie Farrah leaves Arbor a black-and-white composition book. It's the only thing she leaves. Auntie Farrah's already shown her how to divide her life up into wedges, hand them out like orange slices to the things they make from the mud of the creek behind the house. There's this free pottery-making class downtown that Arbor's been taking since she could sit up on her own, and she's worked with the river mud before. She knows how to make things. But she's never made a person before.

It doesn't take long for her to give the composition book a try. It's always just been her and Auntie Farrah, and Arbor's not too keen on staying in the house by herself. Especially when she has a choice. There's this sort of sticky loneliness that webs everything together after Farrah's gone, gums them to each other like it's trying to make sure nothing else gets out. Arbor leaves for work with it on her clothes.

For the next few weeks, she works. There are a lot of diagrams in the book Auntie Farrah leaves her, ones that focus on building legs and arms and ears. They stretch and twist the body like it's something to be crumpled between pages. It—*that*—makes her so uncomfortable that she duct-tapes the journal to the wall above the headboard of the bed she works on, keeps it open so that each appendage is given some stillness. It's Auntie Farrah's room, free space now.

She works till her back aches and her eyes water, till pops of dirt touch down on her forearms like a rude mist. When she falls asleep on the floor, because she hardly sleeps in her own bed these days, the taste of the mud is so heavy in her mouth that she wakes up hacking. She misses the one college class she's still taking—hotel management—but she wants to do this.

It takes her almost a month to build out its torso, the beginning of its thighs, its arms and shoulders. Sometimes she has to break off finished pieces and redo them.

Arbor gives her friend a wide forehead, and she thinks she's seen a woman with one just like it at the downtown Walmart before, but there's no way to be sure. The face is lumpy and one eye is bigger than the other, but it is not misshapen. She doesn't know how to make hair from the mud, and there are no instructions in her Auntie's book, so she doesn't try it. She checks the fingers again, the toes, makes sure that they're long enough.

Arbor finishes in the middle of the day. A Sunday that makes her feel misplaced, like she should be at church even though she probably hasn't been since she was a baby (Auntie Farrah once told her that her birth parents were Methodists). Auntie Farrah used to tell Arbor that she didn't like how wobbly it all was, didn't think that the prayers did anything but ping around in your own head, raw peas bouncing against an aluminum bowl.

Arbor pulls back to look at her finished friend. One of their ankles bends outwards, like the crooked leg of a bobby pin.

She has to wake them up now. Auntie Farrah wrote all about that, too, in the first pages of the journal. You don't need much to wake up something that doesn't need to breathe—Auntie Farrah taught Arbor how to make her own clay toys when she was little, tiny bears and dogs and dragons that would chase her up and down the hall until Auntie called her in to get her hair braided. They were more like windup toys, like those jack-in-the-boxes or those spinning ballerinas—nothing but movement. They don't need much of you, just the piece of your consciousness and your life that you decide to give.

Auntie Farrah told her that she's no guest in her own body: she lives in it and it's hers. And Arbor started to think of herself as a packed house with something wild and sharp and life-giving in every corner. She could wake up those breathless things with the plaster from the roof of her mouth, the flakes of tile tucked into her nail beds.

But the directions in the journal Auntie Farrah leaves her talk about something else. Talk about feeling a body shift and pull under you as its chest gets swollen with brand-new breath. Feeling it warm itself, its blood a stovetop fire, as the clay smooths out and softens into skin.

And the book tells her that it's not just a psychic thing. She can't just *imagine* breaking off pieces of herself to share. It embarrasses her, reading about the physical tokens you have to use to bring a body to life—piss and mucous and other things she skips over because she can't stand to read them out even within the dead-bolted quiet of her own head.

But there's spit, too. She can do that one.

She puts a knee on the bed and leans forward over her friend, tries to ignore how uncomfortably the plastic bag that she'd laid out on the bed clings to her thigh. Gives saliva seconds to well up under the thick ledge of her tongue. And as it's dripping past her lips onto her friend's chin, she decides to think of it as water because that's easier. Because she likes to think that the wet frothy beads sliding across her friend's closed eyelids are nothing but the spin-offs of a geyser, pluming hot and barely solid up her throat.

Arbor doesn't know what she expects—maybe for their eyes to pop open like they're on some NBC soap opera, waking up from a coma to find out that their father is really their brother—but nothing happens. Their face is still, and Arbor's saliva is drying.

She leaves the room, showers with the water so cold each hit of it snatches at her back like the beak of some pliers. She checks her phone for any calls from unknown numbers. Auntie Farrah has never had a phone—she's always been one of those people that can just sit on news, a broken bone or the rapture be damned—but she could call from a pay phone or somebody else's line. It could happen, so Arbor always checks.

It's when Arbor's dressed in her sleep clothes and walking towards the kitchen to grab some water that she hears it. Three sneezes that sound just like the muted rasp of those blow-darts neighborhood kids use to spear iguanas at the pier. Then a heavy groan.

"Ughhh, is this . . . is this spit?"

When Arbor walks in, slow, her friend is sitting up on the bed. And they're not a talking clay-mold, nothing out of a stop-motion animated feature. That's what Arbor had been expecting. That's what her toys always were, what the cups and bowls that Auntie Farrah liked to keep (Farrah always seemed to find it funny) always were. And of course the book had said that the exterior cast would stretch itself out into skin. *Real* skin, flecked with pores that would make it look like some careful, obsessive sketch artist dappled it in pen ink. Arbor definitely hadn't made those dots. Where'd they come from?

When her friend turns to look at her, Arbor's alarm chews away at her heavy shock so well that she finds her feet light enough to run out of the room. She ignores the impulse though, even when it tells her, "Hey, you would *definitely* make it down the street in about twenty seconds if you sprinted out of here right now."

There's no white in her friend's eyes. They're nothing but ill-lit amber iris, the color of an avocado pit. Their face is normal, jaw just a little too sharp but in that pretty way no one ever seems to mind. Arbor has no idea how she ever managed to get their head that perfectly round.

It feels painful in a bizarre sort of way, to be under somebody else's eyes again. Like her muscles are working overtime to make her worth seeing, cords in her back pulling her up to stand straight, calves fighting against her knock-knees. It's nothing like when she delivers the mail or goes to the class she audits. It's not even like when she drops off Cherif Hidalgo's packages and he walks out of his house with his robe half open and a too-wide smile on his face for her. She's sore under this look.

Her friend narrows their eyes at her. "Did you spit on me?"

Arbor's too surprised to respond. Her friend sighs long.

"Did you at least name me?"

Arbor looks back at them. "No, I . . . I couldn't think of anything."

They're smiling a little bit, and Arbor sees that their teeth are white as naked sea salt—how does that work?

"Oh, come on! I'm sure you can think of something."

Arbor thumbs through some memories, relieved when her mind settles on something. The barest scene from a *Days of Our Lives* rerun.

"Lee? How's Lee?"

Her friend leans against the headboard, thinks for a moment.

"I like it! It's definitely not like one of those place names, like America or India . . ." Are they baiting her? Arbor's confused. They look at her for a moment. "You have a place name, don't you." It's not a question.

"It's Arbor."

Lee laughs. "Is your middle name a zip code?"

Arbor doesn't want to rise to it but she can't help herself. It's been so long since somebody clowned her. She's out of practice.

"What's wrong with place names?"

"They're corny."

It sounds like something Arbor might say, if she was braver with herself. It feels a bit like Lee is tickling at the back of her mind, drawing out the things that would never leave her mouth. It makes Arbor pause, confused. The journal hadn't said anything about a mental connection, and it certainly doesn't *feel* like there's some-body else riding passenger-side in her head.

Arbor's not quite sure *what* to do. On the one hand, it fucking worked! She molded the mud and followed Auntie Farrah's instructions and now the outturn is sitting up in bed, talking to her. Getting on her nerves a little, sure, but talking to her.

"Do you want something to wear?"

Lee laughs again. "No. But you can go ahead and throw me whatever you have, if you want."

When Lee gets up from the bed Arbor notices that they have a limp, because of their crooked ankle. She tries not to let it stick with her but it does, raps at her like knuckles on a jangling iron fence. *Look what you did.*

They're a little short, too, although Arbor's hardly one to talk. She'd stopped growing at fourteen, still gets carded for NyQuil sometimes.

Lee waits for her to leave the room, like she means to follow her, but Arbor hesitates. Lee rolls their fruit-pit eyes.

"Relax a little." When Arbor doesn't say anything or move, a little too unnerved to do either, Lee walks ahead of her. Stops, looks back at her over their shoulder. "Tell me where to go."

Arbor gives them the first things she can find, a black nightshirt with this logo of a laughing dolphin wearing bowling shoes, so big it hangs to midthigh on them. A pair of sweats from the laundry basket in front of her bed. She gives them blankets and they leave. She doesn't even check to see where they've decided to sleep, Auntie Farrah's room or someplace else. Arbor can barely sleep herself.

❧

She didn't go to the police when Auntie Farrah disappeared. She doesn't know if that makes her a bad niece yet. The day Auntie Farrah left she took all her stuff with her. Arbor mostly thinks she went somewhere on her own, but . . . she doesn't know.

Plus there are plenty of things she's seen Cherif Hidalgo do that make it more likely she'd eat the metal piping in her walls before she ever asked him for help. One of them scratches at her all the time, Brillo pad–rough.

Before it came out that the owners were selling codeine from the basement, the Corner Café was one of the biggest spots in Cypress. When she watched Cherif Hidalgo make a dangerous ass of himself there, she was ten.

She and Auntie Farrah were leaving the Café and heading to their car. There was this group of kids a little ways away from where Auntie Farrah had parked, in a part of the lot that was mostly empty. They were teenagers, definitely older than her. The final spurts of daylight that gushed past power lines and tree branches found them where they stood laughing, listening to something with a tick-tocking Caribbean pulse. Daylight broke into the kids wherever it could—the thin skin at the shell of their ears, the tops of their cheeks—and lit them up till everyone there, from kids deep brown like Coca-Cola in its glass bottle to kids copper brown like pennies, looked like they rose in the east and set in the west.

Cherif Hidalgo came from behind the Café's mini playground section, rounded the duck-shaped seesaw where it stood hushed and unmoving on one coiled leg. He was in Bermuda shorts and flip-flops, already stroking the gun at his hip like it was the head of some big cat. Arbor thinks he was waiting for a sandpaper tongue to ease out of the barrel to lick at his fingers. It was always with him then. She and Auntie Farrah used to see him all the time at the Café, when they went. He'd put the gun on the table next to his food. One time, she even saw him mistake it for a napkin. They were sitting close enough for Arbor to see how the handle came away sticky with pancake syrup.

His jaw was already tight when he walked up to the group. He spoke to exactly one person. A boy with deep brown dreads that rolled across his back with each breath he took, had Arbor thinking of those long candles they use in the dinner scenes of every Christmas movie.

They couldn't have spoken for more than two minutes before Cherif Hidalgo was wrenching his gun from its holster. The boy, and everyone else, jerked back.

"Why can't you listen?" Arbor only heard it because he yelled it. "Why can't you listen?"

He shot at the ground at their feet. The teenagers were far away enough, that part of the lot empty enough, that it didn't hit any of them. Only bounced back and caught Cherif Hidalgo in the leg. The first time she ever heard the word "motherfucker," in a screech packed up with pain, was when Cherif Hidalgo fell down from the hurt and shock of his self-inflicted bullet wound. Auntie Farrah was already pulling her away, pulling her back, as Arbor told her (because her auntie *needed* to know),

"Auntie, he's bleeding wrong."

He had to be. In the TV shows she used to watch in secret, after Auntie Farrah went to bed, the blood came out hard and mad when somebody got shot. But Cherif Hidalgo's blood came out thin and shy, trickled down his leg in these cords that looked like red drawstrings.

Auntie Farrah almost lifted her up off the ground, trying to get the both of them back to their car as fast as she could. But Arbor saw it. He shot some more, shaky, like the gun was bucking in his hands. He hit the seesaw duck right between the eyes as they drove away.

Sometimes Arbor still dreams about that. Auntie Farrah throwing her arms around her, holding her close, towing Arbor away with her.

❦

Arbor's workdays start early. Of course she has an alarm clock but it's usually her next-door neighbor's NutriBullet that wakes her, the round grinding sound that wheels itself right out of Miss Dawn's kitchen and into her room. Auntie Farrah used to have one just like it but Arbor broke it years ago when she tried to blend her mini Snickers bars into chocolate juice.

Usually Miss Dawn's NutriBullet wakes the woman's baby which wakes her terrier and then . . . Arbor's up, watching the sun pick past sleepy clouds to take its seat for the day.

But today it's a sound like splitting glass that yanks Arbor loose from sleep. Her clock reads 6:00 a.m., a whole hour before she, Miss Dawn, and the baby are usually up. She's scrambling out of bed half-awake still, almost crashes headfirst into her TV.

As she's rushing down the hall there is another sound, too, one that dribbles in through her ears wet, like something big and invisible is drooling it into her. It is high, impossible to miss, two steps down from what she assumes a dog whistle sounds like to dogs. But it's restless. It has hitches, and variations, and . . . hiccups?

Is that crying?

When she gets to the kitchen she can't quite make sense of what she's seeing, not all at once. Her head catalogs the scene element by element like rungs on a ladder: there are pieces of dark broken glass on the blue checker-print linoleum, scattered around the legs of the breakfast table. A whole box of Cinnamon Toast Crunch is tipped over on the counter, bits of cereal shaped like keyboard keys streaming onto the floor. Lee is kneeling on the counter, looking down at Arbor with wide eyes and their hand still clutching the knob of a vertical cabinet's door.

After big hurricanes down here every conscious thing's mind is chafed to hell, on edge. In the wake of them there would be these strange sounds in their backyard that Arbor and her aunt would investigate themselves because the power lines were down and all their neighbors were busy enough reorienting post-storm. More often than not those sounds would turn out to be squirrels, just as rattled about the fallen trees in their backyard as they were. Auntie Farrah's electric lamp would catch them in a palpitating, warped disk of loud white light, and their eyes would look all the bigger for it. That's what Lee looks like right now.

"Uhh . . . good morning? I got hungry but I didn't want to wake you up and—"

Arbor doesn't know how she's been ignoring it this long. The sharp ringing sound is still going, even stronger now that she's in the kitchen and . . . oh shit, she's an idiot. She gets closer to the broken shards near the table, kneels down and picks them up. The bowls and mugs are shattered. She feels it while she hears it, the *squealing crying irritation* and a slight thudding ache that spreads through her palms, reminds her of what a tooth feels like when it needs to be pulled out.

"Is that sound . . . that's them?"

"Yeah," Arbor says, shifting the shards around a bit in her hands. "This is always a risk, since it dries as clay . . . they're actually pretty fragile, just like mugs from a store."

Arbor hears shifting, and soon Lee is kneeling down next to her, staring down into her hand. They look up at her, eyes still wide.

"You can fix it though, right?"

Arbor raises a brow at them, shifts the shards around meaningfully. "Uhm? You see this, yeah?"

Lee rolls her eyes, and Arbor's stuck on the movement. So fluid, natural. Amazing.

"I'm not asking you to whip out a roll of Scotch tape and get to sticking. I'm just . . . like, you know how to do stuff like this. So you can fix it."

Arbor frowns, considering. She's never tried to do anything like that before. When her mud toys broke Auntie Farrah would just throw them away and let her make more. But then again they'd never screeched like this. She has an idea that she's not sure will work, thinks that maybe she could return the dishware to its place of origin. Let it . . . *rest*, she guesses? But—

"I have work soon."

"Have a heart, Ann Arbor!"

"What I'm *trying* to have is a house to live in." Arbor doesn't mention that her shift doesn't even start for another hour. The river's only about a fifteen-minute walk into the woods behind them.

Lee squints at her. "So when's the screaming gonna stop? When one of your neighbors calls in about the corgi you're torturing in your kitchen? You know when white people think you're fucking with a dog they'd run you into the ocean in their Crocs if they could. And the cops they summon would barely be able to stop themselves from helping."

Arbor's stunned again. She was in too much shock last night to *really* think about it, but now she remembers how Lee had mentioned India and America so casually, like it was nothing.

"How do you know all of that?"

Lee frowns. "All of what? Stop stalling."

Lee's fruit-pit eyes still make Arbor uneasy. She's looking at their smooth bald head when she says yes.

Arbor wraps the pieces up in the thickest towel she can find at the back of her closet, to muffle the noise. Watches Lee where they're standing right outside her bedroom door with a regular bowl full of milk and cereal, munching away while they wait for Arbor. Watches the thin fingers of their hand shift smoothly to grip the handle of their spoon and remembers when she'd made them, when they were just static, drying mud. Something clogs her throat. She's ashamed.

"Hold this," she says, barely gives them enough time to grab the bundle before she's heading back to the kitchen.

She climbs onto the counter and throws the cabinet doors open, looks for the other bowls and cups. She finds them, puts them down next to her so she can clamber back to the floor.

"There were more."

Arbor swallows as she grabs a trash bag, starts to pile them in. "Uh-huh."

"That's so weird, you guys just . . . kept them? And ate from them?"
Arbor doesn't like Lee's voice. "I never did."

Before Lee can say anything else Arbor's taking the bundle from
them, grasping the garbage bag tight, and power walking to the
back door. Nudging a pair of sandals in Lee's direction.

Lee doesn't say anything the whole walk there. Arbor breaks off
into a set of thick trees, and it's only Lee's steps behind her crush-
ing dead leaves and twigs, just barely out of sync with her own like
they're actually a single thing walking and time is just lagging, that
let her know they're still there. It makes Arbor feel like she's caught
up in the center of a prolapsing moment, like the seconds skid from
lane to lane so fast that sometimes they actually roll over themselves, make present people plop down onto future people plop
down onto folks from the past. She doesn't like it.

It's an easy path, even though there's no distinguishable trail. So
it's impossible for Arbor to ignore how right now, Lee is nothing
but a moving silence at her back, thick through with blood and
flesh but quiet all the same.

They get to the river and it is as beautiful as it always is. Fast and
foaming, rushing noisy while pear-green frogs hop and play next
to it.

Being in the mud feels just like it always does—like she's in the
company of a boundless, unfenced light, something just like those
beams that sprawl across the savanna of space till they hit the hard
curve of a planet and have no choice but to stop. When Arbor
shares herself, she is the hard curve. Light is nothing but pure energy, after all. She has to gift it something from the house of her,
condense it into something living. That's how this happens.

Arbor crouches down and unwraps the towel first, lays it across
her thighs while she takes up the pieces, careful as anything. She
feels ashamed again. Why did Auntie Farrah ever find this funny?
To keep these things like this?

She doesn't turn back to look at Lee once as she does it, just tucks all the shards into the mud, and then the cups and bowls she brought too. For a moment, all of the objects just sit on the surface. Then they sink, like stones in water, until the mud is just as even as Arbor had found it. She swallows.

A few feet in front of her, there's a gecko that jumps into the mud. The mud wraps around its tail, tries to drag it back. Arbor's never seen anything like it before. She digs her hand into the mud to coax it into releasing the gecko, but it doesn't work. It's like her sway is weaker than it's ever been. The mud gets agitated on her end too, tugs at her shoelace. Lee comes forward and crouches down beside Arbor and digs their hand into the wet dirt. The mud listens to Lee in a way it's never listened to Arbor, like they're kin (which, Arbor supposes, is true). Half a second later, the gecko is free, loping off into the brush.

Lee is smiling.

🐍

Arbor's in a good mood for work that day, but of course it doesn't last.

Arbor's not afraid to say it, okay? (Well, to anyone but her boss.) She's skipped Cherif Hidalgo's house before on her route, when he was lounging on his porch shirtless or watering his plants in a robe way too short for her liking. And she has *every* intention of doing it again, but he's complained about her to her supervisor twice already. If she skips him again they'll suspend her.

She knows what kind of man Cherif Hidalgo is. Recognizes that he's more lenient with her than she's ever seen him be with anyone else. It leaves a sour taste in her mouth.

She gets out of the truck and stuffs his mail into the receptacle at the front of his lawn, three regular letters and some lumpy, misshapen thing wrapped up in pineapple-yellow packaging. His lawn is still empty, so far so good.

But as Arbor is still struggling with the last parcel, she hears the front door open. When she looks up, he's in a paper-thin shower robe that makes her think of a hospital gown worn backwards. He's wearing a gold chain and his chest hair curls over it like it's trying to get a good grip, like at any moment at all it might snap it from his neck. He looks like a Dollar Store pimp.

She notices something dangling out of his robe, limp against his leg.

He grins at her with teeth white as limestone.

"I missed you, love. Will you drink with me today?"

Arbor trips back into the driver's seat of her truck in her rush to get away. She thinks about it all day, and if she could, she wouldn't leave the truck for the rest of her shift. Just toss everybody's shit onto their walkways and wish them the best of luck with it. Like she's done with Cherif Hidalgo before.

꩜

She's not sure what she expects to find when she comes back to the house after work.

Miss Dawn's younger brother Orion used to live in town before he took up this nude calendar modelling gig in New York. When Arbor was around nine or ten he'd ride down their street on this neon-blue motorcycle, engine snarling loud enough to scare the soul out of anybody within a half-mile radius. The sound used to grate on Farrah's nerves so much she would end her dominoes games with Arbor early, go off to watch TV or crochet. And her Auntie worked such long hours at the steakhouse uptown. Arbor only really got to see her during mud-making and dominoes. So one day, when they were sitting at the kitchen table with the pieces laid out between them, Arbor got up just as she heard the growing sound of the motorcycle engine getting closer. Got the front door open before her Auntie could do much of anything, and ran out into the middle of the street.

She stood there. Doesn't remember being scared, just irritated. The bike came careening down the road towards her, stopped so close to her she could feel its hot breath on her bare legs like a panting thing. The rider had tight curly hair and a square jaw.

"Do you always gotta be that loud?" she'd wanted to know.

And he'd laughed, straight gleaming teeth where she could see, like they were old friends. When she got back into the house Auntie Farrah made her promise she'd never do anything like that again, her mouth pulled into a line as hard and straight across as a median strip.

Orion left for New York a few days later. Arbor was coming home from school when she'd seen him loading some suitcases into the bed of Miss Dawn's Chevy. He'd waved to her before he got in the passenger's seat.

A lot of people think that because Arbor's quiet, that means she's careful. Auntie Farrah knew better, knew that *careless* was always easier to find when it's noisy, but you've gotta look for it all the same, every time.

So Arbor's kicking herself a little bit for leaving Lee, a perfect stranger barely a day old, alone in her house. When she gets inside she half-expects fires in every room, ripped up wallpaper . . . maybe Lee's fallen apart somehow like the dishware from this morning and that makes her anxious enough to shove through the door.

She hears the *Sanford and Son* theme song blaring louder than it's ever played from the center of the house. The volume must be on the highest setting. When she follows the song she sees Redd Foxx reading a newspaper in his rocking chair on screen, but the living room is empty. So is Farrah's room, when she goes to check.

She finds Lee perched on the edge of her bed with a textbook on their lap. They shift, and Arbor notices that it's the copy of *Hospitality Management: How to Keep 'Em Coming Back* she'd bought to make her feel like she wasn't just pretending when she went to the class at the community college. Arbor tries to find something to say about what happened this morning—maybe it'll even land her at some sort of apology—but Lee speaks up first. She taps on the book with a finger.

"You know, if you let me stay in one of these places I wouldn't break your shit fixing breakfast."

Arbor's not sure Lee's joking but she laughs anyway.

"Are you kidding? If I could afford that shit at all *I'd* get a room for myself, stick you with this house and the . . ."

Arbor stops. She was about to say something about Cherif Hidalgo from this morning, but she lets it spill back down her throat. Lee picks up her slack.

"You could really leave this house like that?"

Arbor shrugs before she can really think about it. "'S just a house."

"Hotels are better?"

"Sure."

"I read something in here about how some hotel dining rooms have a capacity of like four hundred people. I'm not sure how much you'd like sitting elbow to elbow and getting somebody else's lip sweat in your yogurt but if that's what you're into—"

Arbor rolls her eyes. "Lee. I like hotels to manage. *Manage.* Not to live in."

Lee narrows their eyes at her. "Maybe I don't know what *manage* means. You're already talking down to me. Guess you're a natural at this authority thing."

"So you *do* know what it means."

"Why do you want to manage hotels?"

Arbor isn't sure how to answer the question. She's never had to before. Auntie Farrah worked at the Marriott a few towns over for a year, before they found asbestos in the walls and the whole thing had to be torn down. She'd come home smelling like vanilla perfume and lemon tea, even though she hated smelling like anything at all. It made Arbor think of a full place, with bodies leaning over banisters and squeezing through dining rooms so restless that the tables' hard-sharp edges would jam bruises into their thighs, sloping in against each other so tight that skin held scent like memory. Where the sudden absence of one person was an empty cramping belly for nothing but a few moments, never for long.

"I'm good with people when all I have to do is listen to them."

Lee looks right at her, and Arbor gets that overwhelming urge to look away again.

"Talking's a two-person thing, huh."

Arbor shrugs again.

⁂

The next few weeks are good. Real good. It seems like every day that Arbor comes home from work or her hotel class or her pottery sessions, Lee is fixated on some other activity. There's a day when Arbor finds them on the carpet in front of the TV in a handstand, some yoga infomercial playing across the screen. She comes home the next day with a bright purple exercise mat that she'd picked up from the sporting goods store on her route. Lee laughs and tells her that they're "impressed that she could talk to somebody else out loud for that long." Arbor threatens to take the mat back and Lee tells her they'd sooner take the hands off Arbor's wrists.

Arbor finds them on the couch with Auntie Farrah's old crocheting supplies, has to bite back her impulse to rip them from their hands. Especially when they look up at her grinning.

Arbor finds them with her computer on their lap, about thirteen different tabs open to astrology pages. Her laptop's password-protected and she changes it every month. That's when she starts to really wonder... exactly how much of herself did she give to Lee when she woke them up? Arbor's read about things like this (well, as close as she could get to *this*). Read about the id, the basest alter ego. Read, more specifically, about how it can drive a person to do things their more repressed consciousness would never allow. But Lee's nothing like that.

Apparently Arbor's a Pisces sun but an Aries moon.

"You get mad but it's under, like, plastic wrap," Lee explains.

"I thought Pisces was a water sign?"

"Shut the fuck up."

Things are real good.

So when Arbor comes home from class three weeks later to an empty house, it feels like there's an anvil sitting on her chest. It comes back to her like she's still in the middle of it, that day when she'd walked into Farrah's room to find nothing but a sheetless mattress. When she'd thrown open every single door to every single room in that house as quickly as she could, afraid that if she didn't barge in fast enough she'd miss her and her auntie would escape through a window or an air vent.

She hears a door open and close as she's sitting on the closed lid of her toilet, trying to do something about the lead in her chest. She feels her bones clinking like keys in her skin with the sudden noise.

She rushes out to the back door to see Lee, taking off their shoes.

"Where'd you go?"

"Just down the street." Lee turns to face her and their eyes widen. "Holy shit, you look like somebody stole your mail truck. Are you okay?"

"I thought . . ." Arbor pauses, tries again. "Somebody could've seen you."

Lee raises a brow. Well, where an eyebrow *would* be if Arbor had ever learned how to make hair with the mud.

"Am I an Area 51 sample or something?" Lee looks at her a bit longer, then brings a hand to their own head and rubs it. "Oooh . . . is it the bald thing? Maybe I just have alopecia, people don't know."

"Maybe . . . m-maybe you could wear a wig or something?" Auntie

Farrah took all her wigs with her when she left but, "I used to play a lot with my auntie's wigs when I was little. I still have some of them."

Lee sighs, but they agree to it.

Arbor finds her a curly black one that brushes her shoulders. When Lee sees themselves in the standing mirror next to Arbor's door, they say,

"It looks like I'm sleeping with the pastor but I still share the church program with his wife on Sundays."

Arbor can't help but laugh. Another thing that strikes a chord, another thing she'd probably think but never say, even if there was nobody around but her.

"It looks great."

Arbor gives them a wide navy-colored headband, too, for good measure. It comes down over their browridge and makes them look like they're wearing a bike helmet with the top half popped out. Lee wants to be able to walk all the way to the Exxon that borders their town and Brooksville, their neighbor-town, about two miles out. Arbor chokes on what she actually wants to say—that she'd have Lee pace back and forth between the house and river fifteen minutes behind them, if she could help it—and they settle on the pier instead, a half mile out. Lee likes to go out in the late afternoons, and Arbor likes it because by then all the neighborhood kids who play down there have been snatched back home at the shirt collar by their parents for dinner. They won't get the chance to bother Lee.

The next day, Arbor and the other mail carriers are sorting out their packages at the office after lunch before they resume their routes, and her coworker Mandy accidentally drops a boxy gray parcel. White dust puffs out from it like chalk from the impact. And things go wild. One minute Arbor's getting ready to finish out a regular shift. The next, she and everyone else in the building is being escorted out while an alarm that sounds like a sharp pinging, like a fork against a ceramic cup, sounds overhead. They call the police in for the annual anthrax scare. The year before it was just poorly-packed baking flour. The year before that it was baby powder ... that some laundromat owners up in Ocala were using to cut coke, but that news came back to town almost four months after. In the moment, everybody in the mailroom just thought someone was trying to make an under-the-table dollar on toddler rash.

Arbor's not complaining as she heads home, not at all.

She's in her sweatpants on the couch, about twenty minutes into that episode of *Good Times* where baby Janet Jackson confesses her love for J.J., when she hears Lee come in from their walk.

"Oh damn, you're home already? I told you the old racists down the street could go *one day* without their Valpak coupons."

Lee comes into the living room, stops right in front of the TV, because of course they do.

Arbor looks up at them in mock betrayal. "You live to disrespect me." She sees that Lee's holding the gray sweater they'd been wearing this morning in a wrinkled bunch in their hands, just in their white undershirt instead. One sleeve of the jacket is falling over their forearm.

Arbor nods at the roll. "What's that?"

"Oh, I found him when I was down at the pier," Lee tells her, laying the roll down on the coffee table.

When Lee unfolds the jacket, Arbor sees a nuclear green iguana, ugly as sin, laying on its side with its eyes shut. Its skin is the lumpiest thing Arbor's ever seen, looks like it's stretched thin over a whole bunch of chunky gravel pasted together. Dark blood crusts around a small hole in its mint green belly, rings it like a racetrack. Arbor really wants to dive over the back of the couch, scuttle to the kitchen screaming. But she doesn't.

"Lee, what the fuck?"

Lee looks down at her with wide eyes. "What? I figured you could patch him right up and then I can watch you make chicken again while I talk about your cheese-string legs. Y'know I'm *pretty* sure you cook better angry anyway—"

Arbor's not squeamish, not really. But who the fuck likes iguanas? She sinks back into the couch a little bit and hopes Lee doesn't notice the motion.

"Lee, what do you mean 'fix him up'?"

Lee frowns, uses the edge of a jacket sleeve to poke the thing's stomach. "That's kinda rude, huh? He's not a bike tire—"

"No, like," Arbor tries to make her shifting casual as she pulls her legs under her on the sofa, she really does, "what am I fixing?"

Lee sighs, rolls her eyes, like they're tired of having to spell it out for her.

"You can work your weird river magic and bring him back. The baby sociopaths got him in the stomach, *as you can see.*"

Oh. Arbor understands. Lee blinks at her.

"Lee, I can't." Her eyes flick to the iguana but it makes her mouth fill up with saliva like she's about to throw up. "I can't bring him back. It doesn't work like that."

Lee frowns again. "But you woke me up. Just do whatever you did when you woke me up."

"He's not from the river."

"So?"

"So I can't connect to it . . ." Lee's face hardens at that. "To him. He has to be from the mud, that's the way it is."

Lee is quiet for a long time.

"Oh," they say.

⚐

Lee buries the iguana out back, kneels down and starts scooping up dirt for a tiny grave before Arbor can get them a spade from the tool shed. They go to bed before Arbor does, for the first time ever. They slip off to Auntie Farrah's room without a word.

But when Arbor gets up the next morning, she almost steps on Lee. They're wrapped head to toe in a puffy blue blanket, curled around her bedpost like a halved iris. She's relieved. But the pose, though, makes her think of someone forcefully subdued, and she shakes Lee awake, uncomfortable.

Lee looks up at her from the ground, in her rubbery blue casing.

"Let me guess," they say. "Work again?"

"They can't get enough of me."

Arbor gets up and notices that she has yet to check for the golf club she's been keeping under her bed since Auntie Farrah left.

"Can I come with you?"

"No."

"Pleeease? I'll be as quiet as one of your Amazon packages."

"Lee—"

Arbor turns from her dresser and finds Lee staring out of her bedroom window. Her window opens up right to the backyard, the big oak tree with leafy forelimbs that clench themselves into an awning. Lee stretches her neck, trying to see further down, and Arbor knows she's checking for the grave.

Arbor breathes. "Okay."

Lee walks with her to the station wearing the wig-headband combo. Miss Dawn runs across them in her jogging stroller and almost rolls an ankle slowing down. She has the vein-popping, sunny smile of a woman who can't wait to gossip about whatever she's discovered. Arbor wonders what she thinks she's discovered. Arbor doubts she and Lee look like siblings. Cousins maybe. She doesn't think Miss Dawn can imagine Arbor outside of her isolated bubble long enough to try "girlfriend."

Lee is not as quiet as an Amazon package. But they're not all that disruptive either, and they sit as still as they can on the bench in the back while Arbor drives.

The route is uneventful. Every time Arbor gets back to the truck, Lee's humming a different song, "All Along the Watchtower" or the *Family Matters* theme song or the *Jeopardy!* jingle. It is the most constant noise Arbor's had in a while, and Arbor feels it netting around her, keeping her sturdy. Sometimes, she even finds herself joining in.

She's a bit nervous as she pulls up to Cherif Hidalgo's house, but calmer with Lee here with her. The lawn is still empty as she approaches. She tries to keep the front door in view, but the mailbox is at a deep slant (the dent in its side makes it look like somebody took a bat to it) and she has to lean down. Her bag strap digs into her back so deep that she expects to find a swordslash-shaped bruise across her spine when she checks the mirror later.

She's almost done slipping a thick Humana envelope into the box when she feels it. A finger tugging at her bag strap until it worms under the nylon. It's up against her back now, bony knuckles rocky against her lower vertebrae. Cherif Hidalgo says, like they're elbows deep in some flirtation already,

"Well, this can't be comfortable."

The shock comes first. Then the frantic need to be on the other side of whatever's happening. Arbor twists around so quickly that Cherif Hidalgo's face is nothing but a smudged bar of pale white. She's already committed herself to redacting this memory, gifting herself a blank black space, when she sees Lee. Lee's leaning against the back of the driver's seat. They're frowning, the first time Arbor's ever seen them do it. Arbor notices almost too late that they're scrambling over the seat, trying to get out. Eyes set on some place just above Arbor's shoulder. Arbor runs over and throws herself inside, grabs their shoulders to hold them back.

"Lee! Lee!" Their eyes are brighter than they've ever been, glittering like they came out of the soft ground pressurized. Lee looks at her, still angry and trembling with it. Plastic-wrapped anger. Arbor tries to put everything convincing in her voice when she says,

"Leave it."

"Is this the first time?"

"No."

"Why wouldn't you let me—"

"What could you have done?"

Silence. Lee's face shifts and Arbor kind of feels like she's grimacing into a mirror. Lee looks more like her now, more like what she *wishes* she could look like on purpose. Lee looks up at the cabinets, where the creek mud mugs used to be. Arbor thinks of the gecko. What would've happened if Lee hadn't stepped in. And Arbor thinks of the iguana, almost can't believe that this is the same Lee who'd been devastated to find out that Arbor couldn't bring it back. But the shift doesn't scare her. It doesn't even feel like a shift, really. Two things can be true at the same time.

Lee turns back to her. Arbor means to say no, to the unspoken question and the thing beneath it. But she says nothing. Next door, Miss Dawn's NutriBullet starts up, strange for this time of night.

The next day, Arbor swallows back her bile and smiles at Cherif Hidalgo. She waves to Mrs. Hidalgo as the woman pulls out of her driveway. Arbor invites him to a more private place, and he grins back at her. She's struck by the impulse to embellish the invitation, and gestures towards Lee in the truck for good measure. Lee waves back. She's wearing an expression you could throw on pudding cups to sell them, sweet as pie.

Lee sits cross-legged in the creek mud. Even though it's nearly midnight, the darkness is sheer as mesh. Arbor's view is clear as she watches some branches in front of her shuffle. Then Cherif Hidalgo emerges, Bermuda shorts and all. Arbor's lingering hesitance disappears as soon as she sees how excited he is. Auntie Farrah never liked Cherif Hidalgo much. Maybe she'd approve. Lee nods at her, the signal, and she speaks.

"We were starting to think you wouldn't come."

Cherif Hidalgo comes closer, unconcerned with the mud he's stepping into. He smirks at Lee, then turns to Arbor. Lee sinks their hands into the mud, turns themself into Arbor's failsafe. In case the mud gets too eager at the prospect of this uninitiated stranger and forgets Arbor too. Cherif Hidalgo reaches out for her waist as he says,

"I wouldn't have missed this for anything."

mermaids!

I learn it from watching YouTube videos at the public library.

I'm supposed to be playing math games to put some sense into my head before school starts in a few weeks, but I learn this instead. I show Him how to steal cable, out back behind our apartment complex. We're both going into the seventh grade but he's still small enough to get away with anything, bony. Me, I carry all my growing in my chest and legs. I'm stretched out into suspicious. I show Him how to twist the last cord. We crouch down together, caught up in a mess of wires. I catch our reflection shut up in the window glass beside us and there we are, the slick brown heart of a tumbleweed. We try it for His apartment first, but it doesn't work. So we go with mine.

When my parents are around (rare), we sit on the couch with a stack of throw pillows between us, their borders coming off like skin dying. When they're not, I sit as close to Him as I can. Except for my family, nobody down this block has papers and every friend I've made has gotten sent back. I need thick proof that he's here, thighs talking, arms babbling. I'd knot us at our joints if I could. There is a month-long mermaid documentary on the Discovery Channel and it's all we watch. The tail is the part they really need, the one that lets them swim around living. I am jealous of the mermaids. I keep thinking about what it would be like if what you need the most was always half of you. He tells me he doesn't like it. But whenever His mom comes around with her cigarette hanging out her mouth, calls Him by the name we killed together, the one He still had when she could force him into dresses, His face scrunches up at the TV screen and He watches harder than I've ever seen him do anything. We split everything, Ding Dongs and even our thoughts. That's why when His mama comes around, I know He's mermaid-jealous too.

We both know that the government can send you back for not having papers. But the grown-ups send kids back too sometimes for being bad. It happens a lot at the top of break, June. It happens to the boys who steal ice and Arizona teas from the Kwik Stop fridge and to the girls who roll up their shirts to show their stomachs and roll up their pants to show their thighs, then do it again, then do it again. The last time it happened, to a girl in my grade who got her tongue pierced behind the Beauty Supply, I brought my arm close to my mouth, whisper-distance so my marrow could hear it, and told my body to be good.

There's one day after school when an episode of the show says that everybody out here living, walking around on two feet, came from the mermaids. Here's the proof, they say: if you look down at your belly button, you'll see two itty bitty scars on either side of the button; it's easier for somebody else to notice it. My parents aren't home so we pull up our shirts right there in front of the TV. I think I can see His two itty bitty scars but He can't really see mine. He gets closer, puts His hand on my stomach. That's how my parents find us when they come in from work bone-tired.

He can't come to my house anymore. At night my mom greases me up with cleansing castor oil and prays over me so long I'm asleep by the time she finishes. Sometimes I stay awake long enough to correct her prayers, to remind her that He's a boy (she keeps getting it wrong), and she'll cough like I'm choking her. I see Him in the mornings before school and I tell Him about the episodes He missed. The most recent one talked all about what mermaids eat—the sun, like flowers do. We're standing at the bus stop next to tiny ripped-up Reeboks and Nikes nobody can come back for. "The sun, huh?" He says. We're at the end of the summer, August, so the sun's still so messy that it pours down everywhere nonstop. He opens his mouth up to the sky and it spills in. I open my mouth too. I hope that the light drops down into us. I hope our stomachs become alarms so bright their light is sound is taste is touch. Mermaids! We're so full you can't miss us.

It's harder for us to see each other now because most days my mama calls off early to watch me after school. But a lot of people say I'm only smart when there's tricks in it, so I trick her. Mermaids get away from predators, sharks mostly, by finding rocks their own size and using them as distractions. I have no rocks big like me so that night while the whole complex is sleeping I roll up all of my blankets and some pillows and beat them out into my body. I pull a quilt over my pillow-shoulder. I go to His apartment and knock on the door, loud because His mama works most nights as a nurse and His daddy's hearing is shot from loading ships at the dock. He opens the door and He's coming out already, grabbing my hand like He's got something to show me. He tugs me down the hall, down the steps, out back. We're next to the dumpster in the dark, where landlords throw out all the furniture for the people that don't come home. There's a couch stuck crooked and whole inside the dumpster, raised up above us. It looks like somebody big spat it up. He holds onto my shoulder in the dark and I know He's there. My knowing calms me.

There's a sound I can barely hear because of the cars on the street and the old heads playing dominoes out front. But in the next second I see the lit lighter, see his face, and he lets go to get something else. He takes out a cigarette, one of the long ones always hanging out His mama's mouth. He smiles at me and lights it. "The sun," He says. The sun, between His fingers and in the dark with us. He coughs when He starts pulling from the cigarette but he doesn't stop. My lungs sop up His smoke and I wonder out loud if anybody's ever tried to split papers before. I say it out loud. "You wanna marry me?" He laughs. I'm trying to figure out what kinda yes my yes would be when we hear somebody coming up behind us. I turn and it's my mama, in her robe with her head wrapped. "You unbelievable girl," she says. And if her voice didn't sound so mad when she said it, I'd take it like a compliment and tell her, "Thank you."

I don't see Him no more, but it's for real this time. We barely have any classes together already, because I'm only smart when there's tricks in it. And my mama follows me everywhere, drives me to school, watches me do homework. Whenever she comes into my room, at night, she touches my back to make sure I'm not pillows. She's been asking more and more of her friends to cover her housekeeping shifts at the Best Western. But there's a Friday that comes in September. The Best Western is overbooked and understaffed and nobody cleans like an islander really so they *need* her need her. She leaves and I run down to His apartment. It's been too long since He could enjoy the mermaid show too. He comes and we sit to watch. When mermaids sleep, their human part tries to drag them to the land. They have to bury themselves deep in the sand for any real rest. The whole of them is a fight. I don't like what this episode makes me think about so I lean against Him. And He lets me. He leans against me too till we're laying down, till we're gathered together like fingers in a fist. The TV goes to a Nissan commercial that leaves the screen mostly black and I see it. Us. Spitting up a mountain of ourselves. That is how my mama finds us. She comes back because I'd given her the wrong pair of shoes. The Skechers that pinch her toes instead of the Payless no-names she actually likes. She yells in the Creole she told me she forgot.

My daddy's home from roofing that night. His work's been real busy 'cause the summer's been pulled long, September hot like July, and all the construction happens in the summer. But he's off tonight. He makes me my favorite, the baked mac and cheese I like even though it always makes me a little sad. It's the one that he cooked when he told me my friend Deaven got sent back to Jamaica with his family. Later that night, I hear them talking through my wall. "It would be good for her," my mama says, "discipline." My daddy says, "Is Haiti a punishment?" And she says nothing.

I'm going to spend the next six months with my auntie in Go-naïves. Good for me. Discipline. My mama sees the world in flips, good on the other side of bad, Haiti on the other side of here. The other side of the wrong thing I did, she thinks it's cleaner. Better than the castor oil. For the days that we pack, I don't talk to anyone in that house, not even myself. She watches me even harder now and I can't see Him. I don't watch the mermaid show because my eyes get hot and weird. My mama must've told the school that she's homeschooling me, because that's all the kids there wanna ask me about. He finds me by the vending machines at lunch. Or, that's not right. We find each other. We sit down on the cement with our backs against the machine. I know that if we talk about my leaving, it will god us, force us to rule over our own hurt. I don't want nothing to hurt between us. It's the one thing we've never shared. That day at lunch, we eat from the same bag of Hot Cheetos. Our hands brown and red.

We don't go to our last class of the day—He's good enough to be forgiven, and it doesn't matter for me anyway. We take the 96 bus to the aquarium, shaking cold in our seats, then shaking close till we're propped against each other and warm. The aquarium smells like salt and empty. There are no mermaids here, but manatees are a little similar. I've always liked their people-eyes. There's a display screen at the manatee exhibit, one that spins the earth around and around and tells you all about the water on this planet. He holds my hand. His palm is damp and He smells like Downy. On the display screen, they mark the earth's axis with a dashed line, from up to down. I wish it was solid. I wish it was so solid and me so big that I could grip it like the handle of a knife. Shake everything loose. The countries, then the water. And at the wet root of the universe, we would swim.

Biographical Note

Juliana Lamy is a Haitian fiction writer with a bachelor's degree in history and literature from Harvard College. In 2018, she won Harvard's Le Baron Russell Briggs Undergraduate Fiction Prize. She spends much of her free time baking, because the measuring it requires is the best she's ever been at anything math-related. She splits her time between Iowa City, Iowa, where she is an MFA candidate in fiction at the Iowa Writers' Workshop, and South Florida, where she was raised after emigrating from Haiti.

Printed in the USA
CPSIA information can be obtained
at www.ICGtesting.com
JSHW082101100823
46375JS00003B/5